The Card's Edge

By Avrohom Y Tkatch

ISBN: 978-1-971273-00-6 (Paperback)
ISBN: 978-1-971273-01-3 (Hardcover)

Printed by Candle Publications LLC., in the United States of America.

First printing edition 2026.

CANDLE PUBLICATIONS LLC
17350 State Hwy 249, Ste 220 #32497,
Houston, Texas 77064
www.candlepublications.com

Contents

Chapter 0: The Tower

"Upright, the walls collapse... reversed, the cracks spread unseen."

It was always odd when you felt something wasn't there. Phantom pains, they called them in health class. But the taste of asphalt in my mouth told me the impact did in fact happen. A car hit me. Yet, when I reached for my chest, everything felt like it was in place. It was as if G-d had given me a second chance. I opened my eyes to see if my sense of touch, which told me I was on a bed, was deceiving me. For better or worse, I was not, nor could I decide what to make of it. The ceiling fan spun around, and the bright light of my room was a stark contrast to the darkness of my slumber. I yawned and slowly sat up. Nightmare or not, I had to get ready to go pray.

I stumbled downstairs to grab breakfast, the scent luring me in. But before I could ask for something, I noticed something. Blue shining cards that stood in the center of my family's chest, each one depicting some obscure picture. *Was I in a video game?* Maybe life was a simulation after all, like the heretics once murmured. I opened my mouth again, this time with a different question, when my mother turned around.

"Travis!" She almost dropped her mug on the counter as she ran to me, embracing me tightly. She turned to my father, "See, Nick, the shaman was the right call. He was the messenger." I looked up at my father, and a look of relief and surprise crossed his face.

"Honey, he needs some rest still." My father placed a hand on my mother's shoulder. My mother moved back a little before he asked, "How are you feeling, Travis?"

"Weird," I say as my eyes lock onto the card. My hand subconsciously touches my mother's chest. Her card had the image of a demon, surrounded by fire. My mother placed her hand over mine.

"Sweetie?" She says in her ever-gentle tone. I just stared at the card; its soft blue light was mesmerizing. She then turns to my father and says, "Call him back."

My father and I were driving down the highway in the van within minutes. I glanced at him and the blue, ghost-like card in his chest. The card he had looked like a large water wheel. I wondered what it meant and where I was going as I stared at it.

The gravel path gave me little quiet time as the car bumped down it to a ruined sight. The crumbled remains of a castle now stood before us. A person with a long braided white beard stood there, dressed in a long cloak.

"Nicholas, Travis, welcome," they smiled and greeted us with a soft voice as we exited the car, "to The Tower's Sanctuary. While other shamans may take residence within the city, I admit that nature pulls me to reside here. I find it comforting." I smile, feeling similar. When I was younger, I sometimes ditched a class to explore the forest behind the school.

"Will he be able to take his other classes?" My father asked, his face devoid of concern, though his voice dripped with it.

"Yes," the shaman nodded, "he will." My father handed me a backpack.

"I'll be back with the remaining things you may need." He embraced me and whispered, "I love you." I nodded, and he returned to the car and drove off.

"Come with me, Travis," the shaman placed his hand on my shoulder, breaking my train of thought, "we have much to learn." He led me through the ruins, leaving me to wonder what caused the collapse before asking, "How familiar are you with the mystics?"

"We had a class on general mystics this year," I replied.

"Good, good," the shaman nodded, "now, your parents said you said you felt weird and had an intense look on a person's chest, correct?"

"Yes," I nod nervously. However, if anyone could understand, it would be a shaman, "I see light blue cards with pictures on them." I realize we arrived in a study-like room, filled with books, potions, and a desk. They took a seat on the far side of the desk, so I sat opposite him. Then, the shaman pulled out a deck of slightly larger cards and spread them across the desk.

"Do any of these look familiar?" I recognized the deck as a deck of tarot cards. I nodded as I spotted the demon card in my mother's and the wheel-like one in my father's chests. The shaman smiled as he noted my facial expression. "What card do you see in me?" He asked. I glanced and switched between the deck and the card floating in his chest. I then pointed to a card that read 'Three of Wands.' "Interesting," the shaman smiled, "it appears that you have been given a great gift. I would love for you to study under me to hone this gift. What do you say?"

After a few stunned moments, I nod, "I guess so." The shaman's smile grew, and then they stood up.

"Well then, Travis, you may call me Elias. We shall begin your training in the morning."

Chapter 1: The Hierophant

"Upright, wisdom in tradition... reversed, blindness in dogma."

A knocking sound dragged me out of my thoughts in the shower.

"Travis," a voice called through the door, steady but impatient, "morning prayers, man. You coming or what?"

David never needed to shout. Somehow, even through the door, his tone carried a quiet authority that reminded me of smoke, lingering and impossible to ignore.

"I'm coming," I snapped back to reality. *Today marks 5 years since the crash*, I thought.

The bathroom tiles were cold as I swung my feet down. For a second, I felt my body shift the way it did when I met death, like reality hadn't fully reattached itself. When I opened the door, David stood there in a crisp shirt, tie half-tied, and an expression that made it clear he'd been ready for fifteen minutes.

"You'd sleep through the end times," he said.

"Maybe I already did," I muttered, rubbing my face.

David raised an eyebrow but didn't press. He wasn't the type to chase your ghosts unless you asked him to. "Come on. They're starting without us."

We stepped into the hallway, the morning sun stretching long pale lines across the carpet. Havenbrook College had that strange combination of grandeur and decay, ivy curling along stone arches, stained glass set above modern LED lights. The kind of place that felt older than the Tower Elias trained me.

Outside, the campus opened like a cathedral garden; lawns trimmed to perfection, trees arranged as if by divine geometry. Students moved in quiet clusters, some in pressed uniforms, some in hoodies, all under the solemn weight of routine. Havenbrook had always called itself a university, but it felt closer to a cathedral disguised as one. The whole world did, its laws, classrooms, and prayers all built around the same quiet conviction: that the divine wasn't just believed in, it was studied.

David walked ahead, hands in his pockets, the morning light catching on the silver cross around his neck. "You good?" he asked.

"Mostly."

He nodded, the way you nod when you know it's a lie but choose to accept it anyway.

The bells were tolling when we reached the small chapel between the library and philosophy hall. A few of our friends were already seated inside; Serena Patel, sketchbook open on her lap, eyes wandering toward the colored light filtering through the stained glass. Maya Torres sat beside her, fingers turning a set of prayer beads, expression calm enough to quiet a storm.

David slid into the pew opposite them. I followed. It was strictly forbidden for boys and girls to sit beside each other, especially during prayer.

"See," I whisper to Eli, "still here early."

"Better safe than sorry." He smirks and whispers to me. Pastor Edwards enters, and the service begins.

The service was briefer than usual, as it always was on Thursdays. Pastor Edwards read from the usual passages about faith and obedience, his voice echoing through the chapel as slow as always. I tried to focus, but my thoughts drifted to the sounds beyond the room.

The four of us were the last to spill into the morning light when it ended, blinking as if we'd stepped out of a dream.

David adjusted his tie. Maya yawned and stretched her arms over her head. Serena was already scrolling through her phone, probably checking her class schedule or astrology app. She swore it wasn't accurate, but she felt compelled to prove why.

"Coffee?" Maya asked, already walking backwards toward the cafe. "I can't deal with Philosophy 201 without caffeine."

David sighed. "You can't deal with any class without caffeine."

"That's because caffeine is my religion," she said with a grin.

"Heathen!" I jokingly shout.

I followed them across the courtyard. The smell of brewing coffee drifted from the little shop between the math and the art halls. Havenbrook's Crown Café was a usual stop for us. We passed the worn board covered in half-torn flyers promising everything from debate club to open-mic poetry nights.

We found a corner table near the window. Light filtered through the ivy outside, scattering green patterns across the table. David ordered black coffee, Serena something herbal, Maya a triple-shot monstrosity, and I just sat with my usual: a small cocoa.

"Five years today, huh?" Maya said suddenly, eyes flicking up from her cup.

I froze, my cup halfway to my mouth. "What?"

"You mentioned the date once," she went on carefully. "The accident. It's been five years."

David shot her a look. Serena quietly set her tea down.

"I didn't forget," Maya added, softer now. "I just thought maybe… you'd want to talk about it."

"There's not much to talk about," I said. "It happened. I lived."

The words came out flatter than I meant. For a moment, none of us spoke. The hum of conversation and clinking cups filled the silence between us. Then Serena, ever the one to reroute tension, smiled faintly. "You ever think about why you lived?"

I glanced at her. She was testing me again, seeing if I wanted to share with them what I did with her.

"All the time," I said, before I could stop myself.

Maya reached over and squeezed my wrist. "You don't have to—"

"It's fine," I interrupted. And somehow, it was. Or maybe it wasn't, but pretending had become easier.

Outside, students crossed the yard, their chatter rising and falling like waves. I watched them, my reflection ghosted in the window glass, alive, whole, but never quite the same.

A shadow fell across our table as someone approached us.

"Travis?"

I looked up to see Nate Holloway, one of the upperclassmen from the student chapel devotees. He was the kind of guy who took faith seriously; clean-cut, polite, and probably memorized half the Books of Faith.

"Hey," I said. "Need something?"

He shifted awkwardly, eyes flicking to Maya, then back to me. "Someone said you're... good with advice. That you, uh, can see things clearly."

Maya nearly snorted into her drink. "Oh, G-d. Not this again."

Nate blinked. "So, it's not true?"

Her grin widened. "Depends on what you mean by true. He's our resident oracle. Ask away."

I groaned. "That nickname was supposed to die two years ago."

But Nate looked relieved. "So, it is true."

The word oracle pulled at something in my mind, and for a second, I was back there. During freshman year, music was pounding through thin walls at a crowded dorm party. Maya had been the only familiar face, already a semester ahead of me.

She'd dragged me to the corner where two drunk students were arguing over their majors. "Tell them which one's going to regret their life choices more," she'd joked.

I'd answered something about how one of them didn't want to study law but felt trapped by family pressure. I only did that because the card was within their chests, though. My time with Elias had made me quite proficient in the readings. The look on the guy's face, like I'd peeled open his thoughts, had been enough to make Maya laugh and declare, loud enough for the room to hear, "See? Havenbrook's own oracle."

I'd spent the rest of the semester and the next few years trying to live that down. Apparently, not successfully.

In the present, Nate's hand drifted unconsciously to his chest, as if calling for me to read his card. Not that he could've known. Only three people knew of my power: Elias, Serena, and me. The faint, blue glow rippling beneath his collarbone. The Hierophant, upright: a robed figure between two pillars, blessing two kneeling followers.

"I've been leading the morning prayer circles," he said, voice quieter now. "But lately… I don't know. I'm saying all the right words, but they don't feel like mine anymore. I wonder if I'm just performing faith instead of living it."

I met his gaze. The glow in his chest pulsed, steady and patient.

"Maybe that's the point," I said. "Faith isn't supposed to fit perfectly. It's what you wrestle with that makes it real."

Nate stared at me for a long moment, then nodded slowly. "Yeah," he said finally. "That... actually helps."

He thanked me, murmured something about the next service, and left.

Maya leaned forward, chin in her hand. "You're welcome, by the way."

"For what?"

"For your brand recognition. You think these people would come pouring their souls out if I hadn't called you the Oracle of Havenbrook?"

I rolled my eyes, but she wasn't entirely wrong.

Outside the window, the morning light caught on the chapel's stained glass across the courtyard. For just a heartbeat, I could see faint glimmers of blue: dozens of hidden cards flickering in the chests of students passing by.

“Yeah,” I said softly. “Maybe that’s the problem.”

“By the way,” Maya smiled, “my exchange got approved. I'll be heading to Saint Mark’s for the coming semester.”

“Congrats,” David and I said in unison.

“I get to be the only girl again,” Serena muttered. David smirked.

“I’ll see you all after midterms,” Maya promised. She then turned to Eli and me, “You two, behave.” We smirked, which seemed to make her more upset.

The bell rang, echo rolling across the courtyard like a call to return to the ordinary. Maya groaned, gathering her sketchbook, while David downed the last of his coffee in one long sip. Serena and I lingered by the window as they waved goodbye, heading toward the lecture halls. The light caught on the ivy again, scattering green across the floor. For a moment, everything felt normal: friends, coffee, and morning classes. Then the sound of the bell faded, and the world felt heavier for it.

Chapter 2: The Magician

"Upright, power made manifest... reversed, power misused."

The bell's echo still lingered in my head as Serena and I crossed the courtyard. The air smelled faintly of rain, though the sky hadn't broken yet. Havenbrook had that kind of air that came before a storm; heavy, waiting.

"Professor Marlowe said today's lecture is on aura projection," Serena said, flipping through her notes as we walked. "Try not to zone out again."

"I don't zone out," I said.

She shot me a look.

"I just... drift."

"You 'drifted' so far last week you missed when he lit the chalkboard on fire."

"That was intentional?" I raised an eyebrow.

She smiled faintly. "Apparently."

The Mysticism Department was tucked behind the east library wing, an old lecture hall converted from an older chapel centuries ago. The wooden beams still arched above the ceiling like ribs of a cathedral, and the smell of incense never quite left.

Half the seats were already filled when we stepped inside, students hunched over notebooks, murmuring to themselves or friends. The floorboards creaked like the many prayers had worn them down.

Professor Marlowe, as usual, stood near the front desk, his coat too long and his hair too wild to look entirely academic. He glanced up as we entered, eyes glinting like old glass.

"Ah, Travis, Serena, perfect timing, as usual," he said. "We have new arrivals today."

Two figures stood beside him.

The first was tall, with sharp features and dark hair slicked back like he'd combed it into submission. His uniform fit perfectly, not a wrinkle, not a speck of dust, something David would've been jealous of. But something about how he held himself, still and unbothered, made the room quiet.

"This is Victor Morrell," Marlowe said, "and his associate, Grant Mercer. Transfer students from Saint Alden Academy. They'll be joining us for the year."

Grant nodded politely, eyes calm and unreadable, as if hiding things too young for anyone in the room to know. Victor met each of our gazes in turn, quiet, deliberate, like he was cataloguing us. When his eyes reached mine, something in my chest tightened.

He smiled once, barely.

They took seats a few rows ahead. Marlowe began his lecture on resonance theory, how energy signatures align with emotional frequency, but the words blurred as I watched Victor settle into his chair.

Serena nudged me once. “You okay?”

“Yeah,” I said automatically.

But I wasn’t.

When Victor turned slightly, a shaft of light caught his chest, and I saw nothing.

No faint shimmer, no card, no pulse of blue. Just emptiness.

The absence hit me harder than any vision could. Every person I’d ever looked at had something, a flicker, a mark, even the dull outline of a Minor Arcana. But Victor Raines had none.

My breath hitched.

Serena whispered, “What?”

I swallowed. “He doesn’t have one.”

She frowned. “Doesn’t have what?”

Before I could answer, Marlowe’s voice broke through my thoughts. “Focus, Mr. Calder,” he said from the front. “Your energy’s wandering.”

Half the class chuckled. I forced a thin smile and looked down at my notes, pretending to write. But my pulse wouldn’t steady. Because I remembered something Elias told me, a few years ago, in the dim light of his study —

The night had been cold enough that our breath fogged the air. Elias and I stood outside the ruins of the Tower’s Sanctuary, stars scattered above us like faint embers.

“Travis,” he said, handing me the old deck of cards we used for training. “Tell me what you see.”

I looked at him through the shimmer that always followed our lessons. His own card, Three of Wands, glowed faintly in his chest, steady as a candle flame.

“Everyone has one,” I said. “Every living person carries a card.”

Elias smiled, though it didn’t reach his eyes. “Almost everyone.”

I frowned. “Almost?”

He nodded toward the horizon. "There are some born between the cards. They are neither marked nor guided. No card means no alignment to fate, no thread tying them to the weave of things."

"That sounds... dangerous."

"It can be," he said softly. "But remember that you have that same ability. Those without cards walk the edge between creation and destruction. The cards bend around them, trying to understand something that shouldn't exist."

I turned the deck over in my hands. "So, what happens when I meet another one?"

Elias's expression darkened. "You'll feel it first. An absence. Like the air's been pulled from the room, they can see you, too, though they may not understand what you are." He paused. "If you ever find one, Travis, do not assume they're friend or foe. Watch, before you act."

The firelight caught in his eyes as he added, almost to himself, "The ones without cards rewrite the rules."

Serena's voice pulled me back. "Travis?"

I blinked. The lecture had ended, and the students were already shuffling out.

"Yeah," I murmured. "Sorry."

She tilted her head, studying me. "You saw something, didn't you?"

I hesitated, lowering my voice. "He doesn't have a card."

Her expression changed, a flicker of disbelief, then worry. "You're sure?"

I nodded. "Positive."

She exhaled slowly. "Elias told you what that means."

"Yeah." I glanced toward the doorway where Victor and Grant were leaving, his movements calm, deliberate, like he'd forgotten the rest of us. "It means the deck does not bind him."

Serena followed my gaze. "Then what is he bound by?"

I didn't have an answer.

We gathered our things and headed toward the door. Most of the class had already spilled into the hallway, voices echoing off the old walls. I slung my bag over my shoulder just as Victor and Grant passed by.

For a second, the space between us thinned.

Victor's sleeve brushed mine, barely, but it was enough. The air around him felt wrong: too still, too cold, like sound itself bent out of his way. I caught the faint scent of rain and old stone, the kind that clings to ruins long after the storm.

He glanced at me once. Not a glare, not even a look of recognition. Just an acknowledgment, like we'd both seen something neither of us should name.

Then he was gone, walking down the corridor with Grant in tow, the murmur of conversation swallowing them whole.

Serena touched my arm. "Travis?"

"I'm fine," I lied.

Outside, the clouds had finally broken. Rain streaked the stained glass as we stepped out into the courtyard. For just a moment, I thought I saw the light catch, a shimmer, faint and blue. But it vanished before I could tell where it came from.

Chapter 3: The High Priestess

"Upright, secrets revealed... reversed, truths denied."

A week passed, and Victor Morrell remained an enigma. My enigma.

I watched him in class, in the courtyard, sometimes across the dining hall, but there was still nothing, no shimmer, no flicker of blue, not even the faint outline of a card. Just that same, impossible emptiness. It was like trying to read a page that refused to be written.

He blended into Havenbrook too easily. People liked him. Professors, especially. Even Marlowe, who never smiled for anyone, laughed at something Victor said in the middle of Wednesday's lecture. Something was rehearsed about his charm, like every word was a step in a choreography he'd already practiced.

Serena had stopped asking what I saw. She watched me watch him, and that was enough for her.

On Friday morning, I sat in the café again, nursing a cup of cocoa that had gone cold. Outside, the courtyard buzzed with late autumn energy, students hurrying between buildings, paper cups steaming in their hands.

That's when I noticed her.

Chloe Vance.

She stood in line, hair tied back in a red ribbon, sunlight catching the sharp edges of her expression. I'd seen her before; she was in one of Maya's art electives with the endless group projects. Maya had mentioned her once or twice, something about "a friend who always wins arguments."

Chloe didn't look like she was trying to win anything now. She ordered her drink, turned, and smiled, not at me, but at someone near the window.

Victor.

He sat alone, flipping through a thin notebook. Grant was nearby but silent. When Chloe joined him, the air seemed to shift around them, like a ripple spreading through still water. Victor said something; she laughed, that effortless laugh people have when they know exactly how much power they hold in a room.

I forced myself to look away, focusing on the lack of steam curling from my cup. But even from across the café, I could feel that hollow quiet that came within Victor, the same strange absence pressing against my senses.

The chair across from me scraped against the floor.

David dropped into it, balancing a tray of pastries. "You're staring again," he said.

I blinked. "At what?"

He followed my gaze. "Morrell and his shadow. You've been tracking them as if they owe you money."

"They don't," I said.

"So, what is it, then? You just don't like him?"

I hesitated, watching Victor laugh again, easy, polite, human. "Something like that."

David tore a piece off one of his pastries and raised an eyebrow. "You've been doing that all week. Watching him."

"He's new," I said. "New people stand out."

"Not to you. You didn't even notice when we got a new RA last semester."

I tried to smile. "He's just... too smooth. Doesn't it feel off to you? The way he talks? Like he's trying to figure everyone out before we even speak?"

David shrugged. "That's just confidence, man. You should try it sometime."

I laughed under my breath, but it came out flat.

He leaned back in his chair. "You're reading too much into it. Guy's polite, gets good grades, and makes Marlowe laugh. You don't trust people who seem put together, do you?"

"Maybe I just don't trust perfect," I said.

David grinned. "So, you've never met me."

"Right," I said. "And you're also a shining example of humility."

He raised his coffee cup in mock salute. "Exactly."

The moment passed easily enough, like most of our conversations; quick deflections, humor standing in for honesty. But as I glanced toward the window again, my focus caught.

Victor was still sitting with Chloe. They weren't talking anymore; he was writing something in his notebook, and she watched his hand move across the page with an expression halfway between fascination and doubt. Then, as if sensing me, Chloe's gaze flicked up and stared right at me.

It wasn't long enough to mean anything, but it was enough to make my breath falter. She said something to Victor, quietly, and he looked up too.

I dropped my eyes to my cup, pretending to take a sip. The cocoa had gone terribly cold. I coughed after I forced a swallow.

David checked his watch. "Come on, we're gonna be late for Philosophy."

"Yeah," I said, standing.

We left the café, stepping back into the courtyard. The air had that crisp, metallic taste of early winter. Students moved between buildings, laughter carried on the wind, all of it perfectly ordinary, but it didn't feel that way.

As we passed the window, I couldn't help glancing back again. Victor's eyes met mine through the glass, steady and unreadable.

Chloe turned her head, following his gaze. I looked away first.

We didn't talk much on the way back to the dorms. David hummed under his breath, some half-remembered hymn, while I buried my hands in my jacket pockets, watching my breath fog in the cold. The lamps along the path flickered faintly, haloed in mist.

By the time we reached our room, the building had quieted. Most lights were out, the halls dim except for the soft green glow of the exit signs. I dropped my bag beside the desk and sat on the edge of my bed, staring at nothing.

David tossed his keys into the bowl by the door and gave me a look; not the teasing one from the café, but the kind that meant he was actually worried.

"Alright," he said finally. "What's going on with you?"

"Nothing."

He folded his arms. "You've been off all week. You barely talk during prayers, you don't eat with us anymore, and when you do, you're halfway somewhere else. So, you're flunking mysticism or obsessing over Morrell because you're not telling me."

I didn't answer.

David sighed and sat across from me. "I'm not saying you're wrong, Trav. Maybe the guy's got bad vibes; I don't know. But you've got to stop acting like he's the devil himself. You barely know him."

I laughed, sharp and low. "That's the problem, Eli. Nobody knows him. He just shows up, and suddenly everyone thinks he belongs here. Doesn't that bother you even a little?"

David tilted his head. "People can surprise you. Not everything's a test."

I looked at him, trying to find the words, but everything I could've said would've sounded insane. He doesn't have a card. He's not part of the deck. He's not bound by anything.

Instead, I said, "You don't see what I see."

"That's true," David said quietly. "But I see you. And whatever this is, it's eating at you."

Something inside me snapped, not anger, just the pressure of too much silence. "I'm fine," I said, sharper than I meant. "Just drop it."

The room went still. Eli's eyes flicked to me, then away. "Fine," he said. "But when you stop pretending, I'll still be here."

He stood, flicked off the light, and climbed into his bed.

I lay back, staring at the faint glow of the streetlight through the blinds. The silence settled heavy between us, thick and familiar.

Across the room, Eli's breathing steadied into sleep.

Mine didn't.

Chapter 4: The Devil

"Upright, desire's chain reveals its weight... reversed, the prisoner mistakes the cage for freedom."

It started with another conversation I wasn't meant to hear.

I'd been walking the east courtyard, behind the philosophy hall, where the stone arches still smelled faintly of rain. My head was full of midterms and the low hum of unease that hadn't left since Victor arrived. The air had that brittle stillness that comes when a storm's already passed but hasn't decided if it's done.

That's when I heard their voices.

Victor and Grant stood by the bench beneath the ivy wall, talking low enough that anyone else might've missed it. I didn't mean to stop. My feet did it for me.

Grant looked restless, fingers drumming against his notebook. The card in his chest, The Fool, reversed, flickered faintly, the edges dim and fraying. It wasn't a good sign. Reversed, the Fool meant recklessness, blind risk, stepping off the edge without knowing where the ground ended.

Victor leaned forward slightly, his voice smooth as always. "You're hesitating again."

Grant shook his head. "It's not hesitation. It's... logic. There's a difference."

"Logic's the slow death of opportunity," Victor said. "You can't wait for permission to jump. If you want to live freely."

Grant frowned. "That's not how freedom works."

Victor smiled, minor, patient, the kind that makes you believe you're the one who's misunderstood. "Of course it is. You've been waiting for someone to tell you what's safe. Maybe it's time to stop mistaking fear for wisdom."

The words crawled under my skin. They weren't advised. They were a dare.

And they didn't match the card. The Fool reversed didn't need encouragement; it needed grounding, a tether before the fall. Whatever Victor was telling him, it was pulling the thread tighter toward disaster.

Grant's expression wavered. Then he nodded. "Maybe you're right."

Victor clapped a hand on his shoulder, gentle, almost brotherly. "That's the spirit. You'll thank yourself when you finally stop holding back."

He said it like a blessing, but it sounded like a curse.

I waited until Victor left.

He walked off toward the chapel steps, his coat catching the wind, Grant still sitting on the bench like he hadn't decided whether to breathe again. The courtyard was almost empty now, just the sound of branches brushing against stone and the faint hum of the lights flickering along the path.

I approached slowly, not wanting to startle him. "Hey," I said.

Grant looked up, startled anyway. "Oh. Travis, right?"

"Yeah." I nodded at the empty seat beside him. "Mind if I sit?"

He hesitated, then shrugged. "Sure."

Up close, he looked exhausted: eyes ringed with red, the corners of his notebook bent where he'd been gripping it too tightly. The faint glow of the reverse Fool still wavered in his chest, weaker now, as if Victor's words had pulled it thinner.

"You okay?" I asked.

Grant laughed once, brittle. "Define okay."

"I heard a little of what you and Morrell were discussing."

His posture stiffened. "You were listening?"

"Not on purpose," I said quickly. "Just passing by."

He stared ahead at the courtyard, where the lamps were blinking to life one by one. "He's right, you know. I've been… holding back. Overthinking everything. Maybe I just need to jump once. See what happens."

"Or maybe," I said carefully, "there's a reason you're hesitating. Maybe your instincts are trying to save you from something you can't see yet."

Grant frowned. "That sounds like fear talking."

"Sometimes fear's the only thing that keeps you alive," I said.

He looked at me then, really looked, and for a second, I thought he understood. But the moment passed.

"I appreciate the concern," he said, standing. "But I've made up my mind."

"About what?"

He gave a small, humorless smile. "About trusting myself for once."

Then he walked away, leaving the notebook behind on the bench. The wind caught a page and turned it over. Words scrawled in sharp, uneven handwriting stared back at me:

Cut the rope.

I closed the book and sat there until the lamps buzzed out entirely, the courtyard swallowed by shadow.

By Monday morning, the news had spread in whispers.

Grant Mercer had been taken to St. Luke's General the night before, with a broken arm, cracked ribs, and a concussion. No one knew the details; it was just that something had happened at home 4 days after his conversation with Victor. Some said it was a car accident. Others said his father finally snapped.

I didn't need to guess.

I saw how people talked about it, soft voices, eyes down. I saw how the campus moved more slowly, like the air was bruised.

Serena met me outside the library. "Did you hear?" she asked, and I didn't have to ask what she meant.

"Yeah," I said.

Her eyes searched mine. "You think this has something to do with..." She didn't finish the sentence, didn't need to.

"I don't know." The lie tasted old.

We walked together toward class. My mind replayed the courtyard, the bench, Victor's hand on Grant's shoulder. Cut the rope. It echoed like a heartbeat.

By the time we reached the lecture hall, Victor was already there, sitting in his usual seat, posture relaxed, notebook open, as if nothing had happened. When I caught his eye, he nodded once, polite, maybe even friendly.

And for a second, I hated that he could look so calm.

Marlowe started the lesson, his voice a low drone about ritual correspondences, but none landed. I could only see Grant's card flickering, fraying, thinning into nothing.

At the end of class, I stayed behind. My hands shook, and I didn't realize it until my pencil snapped clean in two.

"Travis," Victor said. His voice startled me more than it should have. "You alright?"

I turned. He was standing a few steps away, holding his notebook loosely at his side.

"Grant," I said before I could stop myself. "You heard what happened?"

His expression shifted slightly, and there was a crease between his brows, genuine confusion. "Yeah. I went by his dorm this morning. They said he's in the hospital. What—"

"He got hurt," I said flatly. "Badly."

Victor's jaw tightened. "How?"

I hesitated. "You'd have to ask him."

He studied me, quiet, cautious. "What are you implying?"

"I'm not."

He tilted his head. "You think I told him to do something stupid."

"I think," I said, "you told him to cut the rope."

Victor blinked, then nodded once, almost to himself. "He asked about his mother."

That threw me off. "What?"

"He said she was getting worse; controlling, angry, said she'd break things when he didn't listen. He wanted to know if it was selfish to move out, to stop talking to her. I told him it wasn't. I told him to cut the rope."

The words landed heavy, heavier than any curse could've.

Victor met my eyes again, and for the first time, there wasn't anything unreadable about him, just regret. "You think that makes me the villain," he said quietly. "But he wanted peace. I thought I was permitting him to find it."

He left before I could answer. He didn't need it either way.

The door shut, leaving only the faint scent of chalk dust and incense.

I sank into the nearest chair, the broken pencil still in my hand. Serena's voice echoed in my head: 'You think this has something to do with...'

Maybe it did. Perhaps it didn't.

Either way, someone had gotten hurt because of advice that was supposed to help.

When I closed my eyes, I saw the card again, The Fool reversed, its edges burnt to nothing.

And for the first time, I wondered if Elias had been wrong.

Chapter 5: The Emperor

"Upright, order protects... reversed, control deceives."

The road from the station to the Tower felt longer than it used to.

It had been months since I'd last seen Elias, and the forest seemed to notice. The path wound through crooked birch trees and low fog, the air heavy with the smell of moss and wood smoke. When I reached the clearing, the Tower waited, thin and gray against the autumn sky, the lantern in the upper window already lit.

He met me at the door before I could knock. "Travis," he said, smiling the way he always did, like he'd been expecting me all along. "You look tired."

"Midterms," I lied.

"Ah. The eternal struggle between curiosity and exhaustion."

The warmth of the Tower wrapped around me as I stepped inside. It was exactly as I remembered: shelves of weathered books, the scent of herbs drying above the hearth, the faint hum of candlelight against glass. Elias poured tea for both of us and motioned for me to sit near the fire.

We just listened to the rain start against the windows for a while.

“You used to visit more often,” he said finally.

“I’ve been busy,” I said. “Classes. Friends.”

He smiled at that, the corners of his eyes creasing. “Good. The living world has more to teach you than I ever could.”

“I’m not sure about that,” I said, though the words came out thinner than I meant.

He studied me quietly. “Something’s weighing on you.”

I didn’t answer right away. I did not need to, because we knew he noticed it before I walked in. But I wasn’t ready to talk about Victor, Grant, or what I’d seen. So, I took the long way around.

“Do you ever wonder,” I asked, “if we can misread the cards? Not in the literal sense, but we could interpret them wrong?”

Elias tilted his head. “Of course. The cards speak in symbols, not certainty. Even I still learn from them.”

“But what if,” I said, “it isn’t the cards that are wrong. What if it’s us, our understanding of what they mean?”

He leaned back slightly, thoughtful. "That's always the risk. Power demands interpretation. That's why you must hold fast to what you know is true."

"What if what I know starts to feel... uncertain?"

He smiled, gentle but steady. "Then you remind yourself that uncertainty is only the shadow of truth. You were chosen to see what others cannot, Travis. Don't mistake doubt for clarity."

I nodded, though something in his reassurance made my chest tighten.

Outside, the wind picked up, brushing against the windows like something restless. The fire popped, sending sparks into the dark.

Elias poured more tea, his movements deliberate, calm. "The world isn't kind to those who see too deeply," he said. "It's why I taught you discipline: to hold the gift steady. Chaos feeds on hesitation."

I looked at the flames, the way they bent and reformed, their shape never fixed. "Sometimes hesitation feels safer than certainty."

He regarded me briefly, eyes soft with understanding, or maybe recognition. "You sound like someone who's seen too much lately."

"Maybe," I said quietly.

He didn't press. That was what I'd always loved about him: his patience. The silence between us wasn't empty; it felt like an old prayer.

When I finally stood to leave, Elias reached for my wrist. His hand was warm, steady.

"Whatever questions you carry," he said, "let them ripen before you act on them. The world will give you its answers in time."

I nodded. "I'll try."

"Good," he said, smiling again. "That's all any of us can do."

Elias stood as I reached the door, the faintest ache in his movement, the years settling heavier on him than they used to.

Outside, the storm had calmed, but wind still curled around the Tower like breath against glass.

"Travis," he said, and something in his tone made me pause.

I turned back. His expression had softened, though his eyes stayed steady on mine. "Be careful who you trust. The gift you carry makes you visible to those who would use it. Especially if the ones you meet are those who walk without a card. Undoubtedly, it will eventually happen."

The words landed like a familiar echo, the lesson he'd given me years ago, repeated with quiet urgency.

"I haven't forgotten," I said.

He nodded once, satisfied. "Good. Not everyone is bound to the weave. Some threads only tangle what they touch."

I almost smiled at his old phrasing, the same metaphors I'd grown up with. It was meant as comfort, but something about it caught differently this time, like a thread snagging against skin.

"I appreciate the warning," I said. "Really."

And before he could answer, I added, perhaps too lightly, too casually, "Especially since I already met one."

The silence that followed was small, but it hollowed the room.

Elias's face went still, the warmth in his eyes dimming to something that looked almost like pain. "Travis," he said, quietly, "what do you mean?"

I forced a slight shrug, half turning toward the door. "Just that your lessons are still keeping me safe. That's all."

He stepped forward, hand half-raised like he might stop me, but the words never came.

I nodded, trying to make the moment less heavy. "I'll visit again soon."

And then I left, before either of us could make it worse.

The wind had stilled entirely by the time I stepped outside. The forest felt sharper, the air thinner. Behind me, I could almost feel Elias still standing in the doorway, not angry, not afraid, just... still.

For a man who'd built his life on knowing the signs, I wondered if this was the first one he'd missed.

The train back to Havenbrook was half-empty, the windows streaked with old rain, and by the time I reached campus, night had settled heavily and coldly. The dorm lights along the quad burned dim through fog, each humming faintly against the silence.

Serena was waiting in the library for what we called 'heavy mystic debrief.' She had feet tucked under her, a half-finished mug of tea on the table beside her books. She looked up as I came in.

"Long day?" she asked.

"Long week," I smiled weakly, dropping my bag.

She studied me momentarily, then gestured to the chair across from her. "You saw him."

I nodded. "Yeah."

"And?"

I hesitated, staring at the mug beside her, the thin wisp of steam still rising from it. "He hasn't changed," I said finally. "Same advice. Same calm. Same… certainty."

"That's a good thing, isn't it?"

"Maybe." I rubbed at my temples. "He said the world isn't kind to people who see too deeply. That I should be careful who I trust."

Serena's brow furrowed. "He always says that."

"This time it sounded different."

She leaned forward slightly. "What do you mean?"

I hesitated. "He mentioned the cardless again."

That made her go still. "Why?"

"I didn't tell him," I said quickly. "Not at first. I just… asked questions. About whether the cards could be wrong. About how we interpret them. He told me to hold fast to what I know is true."

"And what do you know?"

I let out a quiet breath. "That I don't."

Serena's eyes softened, and for a moment neither of us spoke. Her eyes had a calming effect, and I felt I could exhale properly. The only sound was the hum of the radiator and the faint wind pressing against the windowpane.

"He didn't say much new," I said quietly. Leaning back and glancing at the ceiling, "Not really. He looked... hurt, though. Like I'd confirmed something he was afraid of."

Serena nodded slowly. "He's wrong, you know."

"About what?"

"About people like Victor. You saw how he reacted when Grant got hurt; that wasn't manipulation. That was guilt. He felt it."

I looked down at my hands. "Then why did it feel like Elias was right when he said it? Why did it sound true?"

She gave a faint smile, the kind that almost hides sadness. "Because Elias's truths always sound true. That's why you believed him in the first place."

The words sank between us, quiet and unsteady.

Outside, the chapel bell struck once, long and low. The sound shivered through the window glass.

Serena reached across the table and touched my hand, just briefly. “Be careful,” she said. “Not with Victor, with yourself, and with those you trust. Sometimes the hardest person to read is the one you trust most.”

I didn’t answer. I wasn’t sure whether she meant Elias or me.

Chapter 6: The Stars

"Upright, hope guides through darkness...Reversed, obsession mistakes itself for light."

The lamps across the courtyard flickered in and out, their light pooling weakly through the fog. Havenbrook always looked different at night; quieter, sharper, like the world had been reduced to silhouettes.

David and I sat on the library steps, the last of the students already gone. He'd brought a pack of cards, not the kind I could read, ordinary playing cards, bent at the edges from years of fidgeting. He shuffled them absently as we talked.

"So," he said, "what's this about?"

I hesitated, watching my breath cloud in front of me. "You ever get a feeling about someone?"

David grinned. "Sure. You mean the kind where you think they're secretly a lizard person or just not tipping at coffee shops?"

"Neither." I traced a line on the step with my shoe. "The kind where you know they're hiding something. You can't prove it, but you can feel it, like gravity pulling the wrong way."

He gave a low whistle. "You're talking about Morrell again."

"Yeah."

"Man, you've been stuck on him for two months now."

"He's not what he says he is, Eli."

He raised a brow. "Okay, but what's your plan even if that's true? Cross-examine him until he admits he's the Antichrist?"

"Something like that."

The joke didn't land. I kept my eyes on the fog beyond the lamplight.

Eli's grin faltered. "You're serious."

"I just need to know," I said. "Once and for all. I can't keep guessing."

He leaned back on his hands. "So, what, you're gonna corner him? Ask him what, exactly?"

"I don't know yet," I admitted. "Something simple. Something that forces a reaction."

"Travis..."

"I'm not trying to start anything," I said quickly. "I just need to see how he responds when the script breaks."

David exhaled, looking away. "You sound like a detective in one of Maya's mystery novels."

"Maybe I am," I said. "Maybe I just need proof that I'm not imagining this."

He looked at me for a long time, his usual humor fading into something heavier. "You've been off lately, you know that? Ever since Grant. It's like you're trying to solve a problem that doesn't exist."

"It exists," I said.

"How do you know?"

I wanted to tell him about the missing card, the flicker of power that wasn't there, the hollow quiet that followed Victor everywhere, but the words jammed in my throat. I know Eli's not a fan of mysticism; he'd just laugh. Yet, I trust telling him this much.

Instead, I said, "Because I can feel it."

David rubbed the back of his neck. "Okay. Let's say you're right. What if you get your answer, which you don't want?"

"Then at least I'll know."

The lamps buzzed overhead, a single moth beating against the light.

David sighed. “Fine. I’ll help, but only if you promise not to turn this into one of your mystic crusades. Just a conversation. No weird aura-reading, no psychic staring contests.”

I managed a faint smile. “Promise.”

He grinned back, but it didn’t reach his eyes. “Alright, Sherlock. What’s the plan?”

“Sometime soon,” I said. “We’ll get him between classes. Near the chapel.”

David nodded slowly. “And if you’re wrong?”

“I’m not.”

He laughed once, quietly, uncertain. “You sound pretty sure of that.”

“I am.”

But even as I said it, I looked up, past the courtyard, past the lamplight, to where the sky was clearing.

The stars had come out, scattered and cold.

From a distance, they looked like answers.

Up close, they were just burning.

The next evening, the rain had returned, soft, patient, and endless. It tapped against the dorm windows in thin, nervous rhythms.

Serena knocked once and let herself in before I could answer. She always did.

"David told me," she said, before I could even turn from my desk.

I blinked. "Told you what?"

"Don't do that," she said. "He said you're planning something. With Victor."

I exhaled slowly. "It's not what it sounds like."

"Then what is it?"

I turned in my chair. She was standing near the door, arms crossed, her hair still damp from the rain. The look in her eyes wasn't anger; worry had run out of patience.

"Where's your umbrella?" I asked, concerned, as I passed her a towel.

"Don't avoid the question, Travis."

"I just need to know what he's hiding," I sighed. "Once I see it, this can stop."

"You sound like Elias," she said quietly.

That caught me off guard. "What's that supposed to mean?"

"It means you're starting to believe that seeing the truth is worth whatever it costs."

"It is," I said. "If I don't do something, I'll never know."

"Know what, Travis? That someone you don't understand makes you uncomfortable?"

I flinched. "That's not what this is."

"Then what is it?"

I hesitated because she deserved an answer I couldn't give without sounding insane.

Finally, I said, "You didn't see it, the way the air bends around him, the emptiness. And you can't see it. I don't blame you. But, it's like he doesn't belong in the same world we do."

"And what gives you the right to trap him? To prove he's wrong for existing?"

"It's not like that," I said again, quieter this time.

"Then what is it like?" she pressed.

"I just need to know I'm not crazy."

The words came out sharper than I intended, and the room went still. The rain outside filled the silence.

Serena's shoulders dropped. "You're not crazy," she said softly. "But you are lost. You think if you pull hard enough on the thread, you'll see the pattern underneath, but some threads refuse to be pulled."

I looked down at my hands, the faint tremor in my fingers. "So, what, I'm just supposed to ignore it? Pretend nothing's wrong?"

"Maybe you don't have to fix what isn't yours to fix."

We sat in that for a moment. The air felt heavier, like the rain was pressing on the windows from both sides.

When she spoke again, her voice was steady. "If you go through with this... if you try to corner him... I can't follow you there."

"Serena—"

She shook her head. "No. I won't be a part of it. You're chasing ghosts, Travis, and I won't watch you disappear into them."

I opened my mouth, but nothing came out.

She moved toward the door, her hand on the knob. For a heartbeat, she hesitated, then looked back.

"Find your truth if you have to," she said. "Just make sure it doesn't burn everything else first."

The door closed softly behind her.

I sat there until the rain stopped. "Just one question," I mutter to myself.

Chapter 7: The Moon

"Upright, illusion hides truth...Reversed, truth destroys illusion."

For a few days, things almost felt normal again.

Havenbrook had a way of swallowing drama; rumors came and went like passing weather. The rain had lightened by Friday, and even the courtyard felt softer. Patches of sunlight were caught between clouds, and students stretched out on the benches, pretending the semester wasn't already pulling them under.

I went through the motions: class, coffee, chapel. I told myself that I needed space, time to think, and let the noise settle.

Still, there was something strange about the quiet. Conversations would fade when I walked by, not suspiciously, just... slightly delayed. It was the kind of silence that followed a whisper still finding its way through the halls.

David didn't say much. He'd been patient, but it seemed that maybe he was too patient. Sometimes, we'd play cards in the dorm, his version of a distraction or therapy. He'd talk about the Philosophy midterm or Maya's new art exhibit, and I'd nod in all the right places.

“Feels like campus is breathing again,” he said one night, tossing a card onto the pile. “Maybe the whole Victor thing’s cooling off.”

“Maybe,” I said.

The truth was, I hadn’t seen Victor in days. He was around, and I’d catch glimpses of him crossing the quad or sitting in the library’s upper floor with Grant’s old notebooks beside him, but we hadn’t spoken. Not yet.

It should have been a relief. Instead, it felt like the air right before thunder.

That weekend, Havenbrook hosted its winter debate invitational. David dragged me along. The auditorium smelled like coffee and fresh paper, the academic optimism that could convince anyone the world ran on reason.

I was halfway through a lukewarm drink when I noticed her.

Lena Carrow.

She stood near the stage, laughing with a group of law students, papers in hand. Her posture was sharp, self-assured, but not severe. There was something quietly magnetic about her: she’d already measured the whole room and found most of it unimpressive.

I recognized her from campus, though I hadn't realized she was one of the top speakers here.

When she glanced my way, it wasn't long, just a moment too precise to be accidental. Not hostility, not curiosity; something in between.

Recognition, maybe. Or warning.

David followed my gaze. "That's Lena," he said. "Second-year. Law. She's friends with Victor, I think."

"Yeah," I murmured. "I've seen her around."

"She's sharp," David added. "One of those people who could probably argue with G-d and win on a technicality."

She turned back to her friends, laughing again, but the sound didn't reach her eyes.

For the rest of the evening, I couldn't shake the feeling she'd seen through me, not my thoughts, but their shape.

By the time the debate ended, the moon had risen over the courtyard, thin and bright against the clouds. The crowd spilled into the night, voices echoing off the stone archways.

David stretched. "See? Harmless night, no ghosts, no conspiracies."

"Right," I said.

But as we crossed the quad, I glanced back at the auditorium steps. Chloe was standing alone now, phone in hand, her gaze turned up toward the sky.

She didn't see me. Or maybe she did.

The moonlight caught her just right momentarily: pale, deliberate, distant.

And then she looked away.

The next evening, the courtyard was still buzzing when David and I stepped outside. Lantern light shimmered through the mist, catching on wet cobblestones. I thought we'd make it back to the dorm without incident, but then I saw them, Chloe and Lena, standing near the fountain.

They saw us, too.

Lena nudged Chloe and murmured something under her breath. Then they both started walking toward us.

"Travis Calder," Chloe said. She didn't raise her voice, but it carried anyway. "Funny, I was hoping to run into you."

David slowed beside me. "Do you two know each other?"

"Not really," Chloe said. Her gaze didn't move from mine. "Though I've heard plenty."

"That so?" I asked carefully.

She smiled faintly, not kind, not cruel, just sure. "There's a rumor that you've been keeping tabs on Victor. Following him. Asking questions."

David started to speak, but I cut him off. "People say a lot of things."

"Sure," she said. "But this one's not from strangers." Her eyes flicked toward David for half a second before returning to me. "It's from people who've seen you watching. People who think you're waiting for him to slip."

"I'm not—" I started.

Lena crossed her arms. "You're not what? Planning something?"

David stepped forward. "Okay, hold on. Nobody's planning anything. We're just—"

Chloe interrupted, her tone calm and deliberate. "You think he's dangerous."

The words hit harder than they should have.

"Do you?" she pressed.

I met her eyes. "I think I don't know what he is."

"That's not the same thing," she said. "And sometimes, not knowing is the safest place to be."

For a moment, none of us spoke. The courtyard felt smaller somehow, the lamplight dimmer.

Lena finally sighed. "Look, I get it. You've got your instincts. But Victor doesn't need people treating him like he's contagious. He's had enough of that for one lifetime."

Her voice softened just slightly. It was the first time she sounded less like an accuser and more like someone tired of defending a friend.

Chloe's tone stayed measured. "We're just asking for space, Travis. That's all."

I nodded slowly. "Space. Got it."

She studied me a moment longer, like she was making sure I understood the weight of what wasn't being said. Then she turned, walking off with Lena beside her.

When they were gone, David let out a low whistle. "Well. That was fun."

I didn't answer. I just watched the direction they'd gone, the fog already swallowing their silhouettes.

For a second, I almost envied Victor. He didn't have to explain whatever truth he carried to anyone.

"You can have space, Victor. After I get the answer, I'll give you worlds of space."

Chapter 8: Justice

"Upright, truth demands balance...Reversed, balance becomes vengeance."

Morning came gray and soundless. The kind of light that made the world look washed clean and still unfinished. I barely slept. Every hour had played out the same loop in my head: Victor walking past the chapel, the words I would say, the truth I would get.

David found me in the café just after dawn. He carried two cups, both steaming. "You look like hell," he said.

"Thanks," I murmured.

He set the cup in front of me, watching as I didn't touch it. "You sure you want to do this today?"

"I've been sure for a while."

He sighed, rubbing at the back of his neck. "I'm just saying, cornering the guy in broad daylight doesn't exactly scream subtle."

"I'm not cornering him," I said. "Just talking."

David gave me a look that said he didn't believe that more than I did. "Right. Talking." He leaned back. "You realize how that sounds, right? After everything?"

I didn't answer. Outside the window, mist hung over the lawn, blurring the edges of the campus. Havenbrook was quiet, too quiet for a weekday. Even the bells hadn't rung yet.

I took a slow sip of coffee just to ground myself. "He always cuts through the east courtyard after Marlowe's lecture. Alone. That's when I'll ask."

"Ask what?"

"The truth."

Eli's laugh was hollow. "And if you don't like the answer?"

"Then at least I'll know."

Classes blurred. I sat through Mysticism without hearing a word. The chalk on the board moved, symbols took shape, but none landed. My eyes kept drifting to Victor, three rows ahead. He sat with his usual composure, jotting down notes in perfect, even handwriting.

There was something about him, something deliberately measured. Every gesture, every glance, controlled. I should've respected that discipline, but I only saw the space where his card should've been.

Once, his hand brushed against his chest as he leaned forward, and instinctively, I searched for it again, the faint shimmer, the whisper of light that marked everyone else. Nothing. Just absence.

Serena's voice echoed in my memory: Maybe you don't have to fix what isn't yours to fix.

But what if the absence itself was what needed fixing?

When the lecture ended, Victor stood, nodding politely to Marlowe before leaving. He didn't look back. I almost followed, but David caught my arm as we filed out.

"Not yet," he whispered. "Wait till the courtyard."

By late afternoon, the fog had thickened. The campus looked half-swallowed by it, the buildings blurred into silhouettes. We stood by the chapel steps, waiting.

David fidgeted with the deck of cards again, flipping a king of hearts between his fingers. "You know," he said, "there's a reason people talk about letting things go."

"This isn't about letting go."

"Yeah," he said quietly. "That's what worries me."

The sound of footsteps echoed faintly through the mist. Slow. Unhurried.

Victor appeared on the path ahead, the gray light catching his hair. He was alone, just like I knew he'd be. The notebook is in one hand, and the coat is drawn tight.

David glanced at me. "You're sure?"

I nodded once. "I need to hear it from him."

He exhaled, stepping back slightly. "Then I guess this is your moment."

Victor was closer now, his stride steady, eyes unfocused like someone deep in thought. I felt my pulse climb with every step he took.

Elias's words returned to me: *They walk between the cards, unbound to the weave. Watch before you act.*

I wasn't sure which part I was following anymore.

Victor looked up before I spoke, as if he'd felt me waiting. His expression didn't change. Calm, patient, inevitable.

The fog folded tighter around the courtyard, the lamps burning dull halos in the gray.

I drew a slow breath, steadying my voice.

This was it.

Victor stopped a few feet away, his expression unreadable, breath fogging in the cold air.

"Travis," he said. "You've been following me."

I didn't answer. I was still trying to find the right words, something balanced and measured, but what came out wasn't either.

"You hurt Grant."

His brow furrowed. "What?"

"You told him to cut the rope," I said, voice low but steady. "You told him to stop holding back, and then he ended up in a hospital bed."

Victor blinked, genuinely taken aback. "That's what this is about?"

"Don't play dumb."

"I'm not." His tone sharpened, then steadied again. "He came to me for advice. I didn't know how I could know his mother would—" He stopped. "I tried to help him, Travis. That's all."

"Help?" I stepped closer. "You call that help? You told him to break something that kept him alive."

He shook his head slowly. "You're twisting this."

I laughed once, brittle. "Am I? Because I see things, Victor. I see what people carry inside them. Their cards, their alignments, their truths. Grant's card fell apart, and you pushed him closer to the edge."

Something flickered in Victor's eyes, confusion, not fear. "What are you talking about?"

"You know what I'm talking about," I said. "You walk around this place like you're untouchable, outside the rules. You don't have a card, do you?"

He stared at me for a long time, face tightening. "I don't know what you're trying to say."

"I can see them in everyone," I said. "In their chests, glowing faintly, except you. You're empty. You're—"

"Stop," Victor said, voice low but steady. "I don't know what this is, or what you think you see, but whatever it is, it's not me."

David shifted behind me, nervous. "Travis..."

But I couldn't stop. The words poured out like breath I'd been holding for years. "You're not bound to the weave. You don't belong in this deck. You're pretending—"

"Travis, that's enough," David said, but I didn't hear him.

"Tell me the truth!" I said. "Tell me what you are!"

Victor's calm cracked. His eyes blazed with something raw and human and furious. "You want the truth? I don't know what you see when you look at me. But maybe you should start asking what you see when you look at yourself!" He stepped closer, closing the space between us. "You talk about cards, threads, and fate like they make you special. Like they excuse everything. But tell me, Travis, have you ever looked?"

My breath caught. "What?"

"Maybe there's a reason you don't see a card in me," he said, voice rising now, sharp and final. "Just because you have a card in your chest doesn't mean everyone else does!"

The words hit like a blow, and for a moment, the world tilted. The air seemed to pulse, a low hum running through the fog. The lamps flickered, every shadow bending inward.

Then everything went still.

When I blinked again, Victor was gone. So was Eli. The courtyard stretched empty, silent, the mist thicker than before.

I don't remember walking back to the dorm, only the mirror, the thin strip of glass above the sink, catching the dim yellow light. My reflection looked wrong, blurred at the edges, eyes too wide.

For a heartbeat, nothing.

Then I saw it.

A faint glow, deep under the skin, pulsing like a heartbeat. Not blue, not silver like the others. Red. Dark red.

The card was there, dark as fire—

Death.

The thirteenth Major Arcana.

It flickered once, then settled, still and sure in my chest.

I pressed a trembling hand to it, but it didn't fade. The symbol burned steadily, like it had been waiting for me to notice.

In the silence, Elias's voice came back to me; soft, distant, protective: You were chosen to see what others cannot. Don't mistake doubt for clarity.

I didn't. Not anymore.

Clarity hurt.

Chapter 9: Death

"Upright, endings become transformation...Reversed, transformation becomes ruin."

A week passed.

I barely noticed the days. The lamps in the dorm flickered from gold to dark, back to gold again, and I never left my room except to breathe. I never bothered checking the mirror. I didn't want to see the thing burning in my chest. I didn't want to see myself reflected beside it.

Campus moved without me. I could hear it through the window: footsteps, laughter, the faint hum of the chapel bells. Everything sounded distant, like it belonged to a world I'd stepped out of.

David stopped waking me after the third day. Serena didn't come by at all.

One day, David did show up again, this time when I thought he would have been in classes, and it was with his usual lack of ceremony. A quiet knock, then the door creaked open.

"Room smells like exile," he said softly.

I sat on the edge of my bed, eyes unfocused. "Been busy."

"Doing what? Staring at walls?"

I didn't answer. He set down a small paper bag, coffee, and two pastries, which I used to get before morning lectures.

"Thought I'd try bribery," he said, sitting opposite me. "So, you gonna tell me what the hell happened out there with Victor?"

I stared at the floor. "You wouldn't believe me."

"Try me."

His tone wasn't challenging; just tired. Familiar. Like someone asking you to set down a weight, finally, you'd been pretending not to carry.

So, I told him.

Not everything at once. Just enough. The cards, the way I saw them, the glow in people's chests, Elias's teachings. The lie about the cardless. The confrontation. Victor's words.

And finally, the mirror.

By the time I finished, David hadn't moved.

"So, you're telling me," he said carefully, "that everyone has a... tarot card glowing inside them?"

"Something like that."

"And yours is—"

"Death." I opened my shirt a little, allowing the card to shine with its red tint, "for some reason, Victor could see mine. Which now means everyone can. My shirt allows me to hide it, though."

He blinked. "That's... grim."

"It's not about dying," I said quietly. "It's about change. Transformation. The end that makes way for something else."

He studied me a moment longer. "So, this, this power, you've had it since the accident?"

I nodded. "Elias taught me to control it. Or thought he did. Turns out he was just trying to hide part of it from me."

David exhaled. "Well, that tracks. Guy's always had that mysterious old-wizard vibe."

I almost smiled. "You believe me?"

"I believe you believe it," he said. Then, after a beat, "And that's enough."

The quiet between us didn't feel heavy this time. Just real.

After a while, he said, "You know who you should actually be talking to?"

I didn't have to ask. "Serena won't want to see me. Not after what I set out to do."

"Maybe. But she should hear you. Your side, not the lies." He stood, brushing crumbs from his jeans. "C'mon. Let's go fix at least one of your disasters."

The chapel garden looked different in the sunlight. After weeks of rain, everything had the faint shimmer of being newly made: stone paths slick with leftover dew, ivy climbing the walls like veins rediscovering blood. Serena sat near the fountain, sketchbook open on her knees, earbuds in. A graphite smudge ran along the side of her hand.

David and I stopped at the edge of the courtyard. "She's here," he said quietly.

"I see her," I murmured. My voice felt smaller than the space between us.

David glanced at me, then back at Serena. "You sure you want me here for this?"

"Yes," I said. "I think you need to be."

We crossed the grass slowly. The sound of her pencil against paper was soft, steady, like the garden had its own heartbeat. When our shadows reached her, she looked up, tugging one earbud free.

"Hey," she said, wary but calm. "Didn't expect either of you out here."

"Can we talk?" I asked.

Her eyes flicked between us, then she nodded toward the bench opposite hers. "If this is about classes, I'm off duty."

"It's not," David said gently. "It's about everything else."

That caught her off guard. She closed her sketchbook halfway. "Everything else is a big category."

Eli's tone stayed careful. "He told me what happened. With Victor. With you. He didn't mean for it to go that far."

Her expression didn't change, but her hand tightened on the pencil. "You told him?"

I nodded. "He deserved to know."

The garden was quiet except for the soft splash of the fountain. Somewhere behind us, bells marked the hour.

"I wanted to apologize," I said finally. "For how I treated you. For making you feel like your doubt was disloyalty. You tried to stop me from breaking something I didn't understand, and I called it faith."

Serena took a long breath, eyes fixed on the sunlight dancing on the water. "You believed so completely you couldn't see anyone else's truth. That's not faith, Travis. That's blindness."

"I know," I said. "And I'm sorry for it. I didn't come here to defend myself. I came because I don't want silence to be what's left between us."

She studied me for a long moment, the corners of her eyes unreadable. Then she looked at Eli. "And you? Why are you here?"

David hesitated, then said, "Because he wouldn't come alone. And because I saw what he was turning into. You were right to walk away."

Serena nodded slightly, as if she'd been waiting for someone else to say it out loud. She reached into her bag, pulled a fresh pencil, and turned it between her fingers.

"I don't know if I can forgive you," she said. "But I'm tired of hating you."

"That's enough," I said softly.

She smiled faintly, just once. "You always did have a low bar for miracles."

We all laughed; not much, just enough to loosen the air around us.

For a moment, the garden fell back into quiet. The sunlight moved through the trees in shifting bands, and I thought how strange it was that something so bright could make every shadow sharper.

David stood, brushing his hands on his jacket. “I’ll give you two a minute.”

As he stepped away, Serena reopened her sketchbook. “You know,” she said, pencil poised above the page, “I was drawing the chapel earlier. I couldn’t get the light right.”

I watched the curve of her wrist, the slow return to rhythm. “Maybe it’s not about getting it right,” I said. “Maybe it’s just about trying again.”

She didn’t answer, but the corner of her mouth curved slightly. I took that as enough.

A few minutes of silence later, Serena asked, “What will you do?”

I looked toward the horizon, where the tower’s peak barely appeared above the trees. “I need to see Elias. He’s the only one who might know what this means.”

She hesitated. “And if he doesn’t?”

“Then I’ll find out myself.”

The wind moved through the garden, scattering a few of her pages across the grass. She bent to pick them up, and when she straightened again, there was something steadier in her eyes.

“Then I’m coming with you,” she said.

I opened my mouth to argue, but stopped. For once, I didn’t want to be alone with what I’d found.

“Okay,” I said. “We leave tomorrow.”

She nodded, a faint smile ghosting across her face. “Then tonight, you rest. You look like a corpse.”

“Fitting, isn’t it?”

She rolled her eyes, but the laugh that followed was real.

The mirror was covered that night, but I could still feel the pulse under my skin; slow, steady, waiting.

Change had a heartbeat now. And it was mine.

The next morning came pale and silent.

Fog rolled over the campus lawns like breath, curling through the arches and pathways. Serena met me at the station just after dawn, her bag slung over one shoulder and her sketchbook under her arm. Neither of us said much. The air between us was heavy with what hadn’t been said yet, but steady enough to stand on.

The train arrived late, groaning like something old that remembered its purpose. We found seats near the window. The glass was cold against my temple as we pulled away from Havenbrook, the college shrinking behind us, spires fading into the fog, bells echoing until they were nothing but memory.

Serena watched the passing landscape for a while: frost-dusted fields, riverbeds cutting through dark soil, distant houses with their lights still on. She wanted to ask what I'd say to Elias when we arrived, but the words never came.

Instead, she said softly, "It feels like we're crossing into somewhere else."

"We are," I murmured. "We always are."

The ride took hours, but time felt folded, smaller somehow. By the time we stepped off, the sun was already leaning west. The woods surrounding the Tower were denser than I remembered, branches knotted together like ribs, the path thin and uneven.

The walk was quiet except for the crunch of leaves under our boots and the occasional snap of a branch overhead. The air smelled of pine and rain, sharp and clean, almost metallic.

When the Tower finally came into view, it didn't feel like a building. It felt like a memory, taller than I remembered, its lantern burning faintly against the pale sky.

Serena slowed beside me. "So, this is where it all started."

"Yeah," I said. My throat felt tight. "And maybe where it ends."

We stood at the base of the steps. The door was half-shadowed, with the same iron hinges and faint hum under the wood, like something breathing out of sight.

I reached for the handle.

The pulse beneath my ribs quickened, slow, steady, waiting.

Chapter 10: The Hanged Man

"Upright, surrender becomes clarity...Reversed, clarity becomes loss."

Once again, Elias opened the door before I could knock.

He stood framed in the doorway, smaller somehow. His shoulders had lost their surety, and his eyes carried the tired glimmer of someone waiting too long.

"Travis," he said softly. "You made good time."

Serena and I exchanged a glance. She bowed her head slightly. "Elias."

He smiled at her, faintly. "You look well, Serena." Then his gaze found me again, and the smile faltered. I thought he was staring at my face for a heartbeat until I realized his eyes were fixed lower, at the faint red glow pulsing through my shirt.

"Come in," he said, stepping aside.

The Tower was colder than I remembered. The hearth was unlit, the shelves half-empty. Candles burned low in the corners, their wax pooled like melted bone. It smelled of dust and rain, not herbs and smoke.

He motioned to the table. "Tea?"

"No," I said.

He poured some, the soft clink of porcelain cutting through the silence.

"I was wondering when you'd come," he said finally. "You always find your way back when the questions grow louder than the answers."

"I didn't come for nostalgia."

His hands paused over the cup. "No. I imagine you didn't."

Serena sat quietly by the window, letting the conversation shape itself.

I stood. "You lied to me."

He didn't flinch. "About many things, I suspect. Which one are we beginning with?"

"The cardless," I said. "You told me they were dangerous and could bend the weave. That they were like me."

"And now you believe otherwise."

"I met one. Victor. He doesn't even know what I am, and you made me see him as something monstrous."

Elias's expression didn't change, but a faint tremor passed through his hand. "I told you that to protect you, Travis."

"From what?"

"From the truth."

I laughed, a short, cracked sound. "That's not protection. That's fear."

He sighed, the sound deep and weary. "Fear is not always wrong."

"You've been lying since the beginning," I said, voice rising. "The cards, the power, the accident; everything. You said the gift was divine. You said I was chosen. But it's not a gift, is it? It's a curse. That's why the card is here." I pointed at my chest. Serena placed her hand over my free one, calming me slightly.

Elias looked at me for a long moment. The fire that had always lived in his eyes had dimmed, replaced by something quieter: grief.

He set the teacup down. "You're right," he said simply. "It was never divine."

The words hollowed the room. Serena stirred but didn't interrupt.

I took a step closer. "Then what is it?"

Elias looked past me, the covered window, and the faint light pressing through the curtain. "Do you remember the night of your accident?"

"I remember dying," I said.

He nodded slowly. "You did. And when I found you, the deck found you, too. Death had already chosen you. The thirteenth arcana does not give back what it takes."

I swallowed. "But I'm here."

"Yes," he said. "Because I wouldn't let you go. Not after hearing your parents' tearful request. You were so young, Travis."

The words hit like a blow.

"What did you do?" I whispered.

He looked down at his hands, as if he could still feel the weight of that night between them. "I made a bargain."

"With who?"

Elias's voice went softer, almost reverent. "With what lies between the cards. The void that holds them apart. A demon, if you like names. It calls itself Nightmare."

Serena's eyes widened. "You made a pact?"

He nodded. "To bring you back. To keep your soul anchored here. But there are rules to every exchange. Nightmare offered years for years. So, I gave him mine."

My pulse roared in my ears. "You sold your life for mine?"

"I traded time," he said gently. "Not my life. I still had enough to teach you, to prepare you. But the debt comes due, eventually."

I shook my head. "You should've let me go."

He smiled, faintly. "I couldn't. You were meant to be more than an ending."

The red light beneath my ribs began to flicker, pulse by pulse, brighter. "You bound him to me."

"I had no choice," he said. "The Death arcana needed an anchor. You were halfway across the threshold; I pulled you back, but the card pulled something else with you. That's why it burns red now. It isn't a symbol anymore; it's a door."

The air in the room thickened. I could feel the pulse matching my heartbeat.

Elias's hands trembled on the table. His skin looked almost translucent. "He's been waiting, Travis. Nightmare never breaks a promise. He comes to collect what was given."

Serena rose to her feet. "Then we leave. Now."

Elias shook his head. "You can't outrun a debt sealed in blood and breath."

I took a step toward him. "Then I'll give it back. My years, my life, whatever it takes—"

He smiled sadly. "That's not how it works. Death doesn't take. It returns."

The air went still. Then the light inside my chest erupted.

It wasn't heat, it was pressure, soundless and vast. The red glow flooded the room, spilling across the walls, swallowing the candlelight. Serena shouted my name, but I couldn't move. The air rippled like water.

And then the world tore open.

Something emerged from the burning shape in my chest, not fire, not smoke, but absence. The light bent around it, and shadows swallowed sound. It had no face or limbs, only the suggestion of form, a whispering outline that shimmered like underwater glass.

When it spoke, the voice came from everywhere.

"You have carried my promise well."

Elias didn't move. "It's time, then."

"Time is the bargain's weight," Nightmare said. "And yours is spent."

Serena tried to reach him, but Elias lifted a hand, steady despite the trembling. "Stay back."

He looked at me one last time. "You see now, child. Death isn't an ending, it's a return."

I reached for him. "Don't." I felt tears stream down my cheeks.

He smiled. "I'm not afraid."

The shadow reached out, not touching, not striking, just folding him in. The light dimmed, and the world seemed to inhale.

When it exhaled, Elias was gone. Only his cup remained, still trembling faintly.

I fell to my knees. The red glow in my chest faded to a dim ember. The Tower was silent again, the air heavy with the smell of ash and rain.

Serena knelt beside me, her hand on my shoulder. "Travis—"

"I know," I whispered.

There, on the table where Elias had sat, lay a single card facedown. I reached for it with shaking fingers and turned it over.

The Hanged Man.

Suspended upside down, serene, eyes open.

Surrendered.

Outside, the wind shifted, carrying the faint sound of the lantern above the Tower flickering out.

Serena's voice trembled. "What now?"

I stared at the card, Elias' faint outline still lingering in my mind. "He said Death returns."

"Returns to what?"

"I don't know." I rose slowly, pocketing the card. "But we're going to find out."

As we stepped outside, the path behind us had vanished, swallowed by fog. The only way left was forward.

And in the silence that followed, I swore I could hear something walking beside me; not Nightmare, not Elias, but the echo of both.

Chapter 11: The Sun

"Upright, joy revealed... reversed, joy obscured."

It had been a week since the incident at Tower.

The fog that swallowed the woods still lived somewhere in me, but Havenbrook looked almost bright again. The trees around the courtyard shed their leaves of gold, and the morning air smelled like wet leaves and coffee.

Classes had resumed, the chapel bells rang on schedule, and no one else seemed to notice if the world had ended in that tower.

David claimed that was proof the world didn't care enough to fall apart.

I claimed that it was probably for the best.

We sat at our usual table in Crown Café, the same corner by the ivy window. Serena had her sketchbook open again, though most of what she drew these days were lines that went nowhere. David was trying to teach himself card tricks with a regular deck, failing spectacularly.

"I swear this worked online," he muttered, flicking a card that hit my cup.

"It's less sleight of hand," Serena said without looking up, "and more public embarrassment."

David grinned. "It's performance art."

I almost smiled. The air didn't feel crushing my lungs for the first time in weeks. Then the café door slammed open.

"Okay," a voice announced, "who died?"

Maya Torres stood in the doorway, suitcase in one hand, coffee in the other, scarf trailing behind her like a battle flag.

The entire café turned to look, because of course they did.

"Don't tell me," she said, scanning the table. "I leave for one semester, and you—" she pointed at me "—go full haunted recluse, you—" Serena—"develop a tragic art phase, and you—" Eli—"still have that haircut."

"Good to see you too," David said dryly.

Maya dropped her bag beside the table and collapsed into the chair across from me. "I mean, I was gone for four months, not four centuries. What the hell happened to you people?"

Serena glanced at me, her look warning and amused at once.

I said, "Long story."

"I love long stories," Maya said, grinning. "Especially if they involve supernatural trauma or at least a bad breakup."

"Check and check," David muttered. I glared at him. Hard. Serena chuckled at that one.

"Perfect," she said. "Start from the least emotionally devastating one."

We didn't. Not right away.

Instead, we let her talk about her semester abroad, the art professors who wore velvet capes unironically, the canal that smelled like "existential dread and perfume." She filled the air like sunlight fills a cold room.

I didn't realize how much I'd missed her until the noise felt good again.

Serena's laughter came easier than it had in weeks. David leaned back, arms crossed, letting Maya's chaos rewire the air.

"So what did I miss?" she asked finally, slightly lowering her voice, eyes flicking between us. "Besides the apocalypse."

"Define apocalypse," I said.

"The emotional kind," she said. "The kind that makes you write bad poetry."

I met Serena's eyes. "Then yes."

Maya blinked. "Wait; you're serious?"

"Serena burned her sketchbook," David said helpfully.

"I did not burn it," Serena said. "It fell into a candle."

Maya stared. "You two are actually feral without me."

"Accurate," David said.

We walked the campus after coffee. The weather, blue skies, and the warmth that made the cold bearable had shifted. Maya kept pointing out how everything looked smaller than she remembered.

"Did the buildings shrink, or did I grow as a person?" she asked.

"You grew louder," David said.

"Same thing."

I let them banter ahead of me, letting the rhythm of their conversation fill the space where silence used to live. Serena fell back to walk beside me.

"How are you?" she asked softly.

"Breathing," I said.

"That's an improvement."

The sunlight caught her hair, making the air feel almost safe again. But behind that calm, I could feel the ghost of the Tower: Elias's last words, the smell of ash and rain.

Maya turned around and walked backward, grinning. “You two back together or just maintaining plausible deniability?”

Serena rolled her eyes. “Focus, Maya.”

“Focusing! Just asking the hard-hitting questions.”

“Still a journalist at heart,” David said.

Maya winked. “Someone has to record your descent into moral ambiguity.”

By noon, we ended up on the philosophy building’s roof, a place we hadn’t been since the beginning of the fall. The climb was still treacherous, but the view was still worth it. From there, the whole campus looked like a map drawn in sunlight.

Grant Mercer was in the courtyard below, walking with his arm still in a sling.

When he saw us, he waved once. I waved back. The look we shared wasn’t forgiveness, but it wasn’t guilt either. Something lighter.

“Is that Grant?” Maya asked. “Didn’t he vanish for, like, months?”

“Yeah,” David said. “Bad fall.”

Maya frowned. “He looks fine.”

“Mostly,” Serena said.

I watched Grant for a moment longer, the faint shimmer of his card, The Fool, upright now, visible only to me. The light pulsed steadily, not recklessly. He'd learned. Maybe we both had.

That night, the four of us met again on the chapel steps. Someone had brought food, probably Maya, since it was good. We sat in a rough circle, the lantern light washing everything gold.

David told stories from his theology class; Serena sketched us without warning; Maya hummed under her breath, some song that didn't exist yet.

For a while, it almost felt like the world had reset.

"Alright," Maya said eventually, leaning back on her elbows. "So. Honest answers. How bad did it get while I was gone?"

Serena glanced at me. "You sure you want the honest version?"

"Always."

I told her, not all of it, but enough. Elias, the Tower, the bargain. Nightmare. Death. Maya didn't interrupt once. When I finished, she sat back, quiet longer than expected.

"Damn," she said finally. "I miss one semester, and you go full mythic tragedy."

David snorted. Serena smiled faintly.

Maya reached over and placed a hand on mine. "You okay?"

I nodded. "Getting there." I glance at Serena, who gives me a soft smile.

"Good," she said softly. "Because I don't think you're done yet. But lover girl has got you covered." She smiled at Serena, who only looked away shyly.

The night deepened. The chapel bell rang once, slow and deliberate. Above us, the stars cut through the clouds like pinholes in the dark. I leaned back, letting the sound fill the silence. For the first time since Elias died, I felt something close to peace, not because the pain had gone, but because I wasn't alone in it anymore.

Maya started humming again, some tune she said she'd heard in a café in Prague. David joined in, off-key. Serena laughed.

For a moment, the world tilted toward something beautiful.

And then, behind Maya's shoulder, something flickered. A faint glimmer, silver, then gone. A card. Not glowing fully, just phasing in and out of sight like a half-remembered thought. I blinked, and it vanished.

Maya looked over. "What?"

"Nothing," I said. "Just, nothing."

She shrugged, still smiling. "If you start seeing ghosts again, tell them I want royalties."

David laughed. Serena looked at me a moment longer.

The lantern flame wavered in the breeze. I let myself laugh too, quietly, carefully.

For the first time in weeks, it felt easy. For the first time in months, it felt safe. But somewhere deep inside, the red glow pulsed once, soft as a heartbeat. And when I looked at the stars, I couldn't tell if they were shining... or burning out.

Chapter 12: Judgement

"Upright, truth awakens... reversed, truth denied."

The chapel always looked beautiful in daylight. The sun caught on the old stained glass, scattering color across the marble floor. Every hue had weight: blue, for breath, gold, for forgiveness. For once, the air didn't feel like it was pressing down.

This morning's congregation was full. Students filled every pew, some yawning behind hymnbooks, others swaying faintly to the organ's slow rhythm. I sat near the back, where the light hit the stone pillars and made them shimmer faintly like moving water.

Nate Holloway stood at the pulpit.

He looked calmer than he used to; confident but not proud. A year ago, he could barely lift his eyes from the page. Now, his voice carried through the room like something practiced and lived-in.

"Faith," he said, "isn't certainty. It's the act of standing still long enough to listen, even when silence is all you hear."

He paused, looking over the crowd, smiling in that unpolished way of his.

"I used to think belief meant having the right answers," he continued. "Now I think it's about learning to ask better questions."

The organ hummed softly under his words. I felt the room's quiet gather and settle as sound does before rain.

When the service ended, students drifted out in small clusters, murmuring about breakfast and midterm grades. The air outside was brisk, the sun breaking through thin clouds. The chapel bells rang once: low, patient, steady.

I stayed behind. So did Nate.

He was stacking books on the altar, humming under his breath. When he noticed me, his face lit up.

"Travis! Hey." He came down the steps, extending a hand. "Haven't seen you in ages."

"Been busy," I said, a small smile giving the mask and truth at the same time.

"Yeah, me too. Apparently, running morning prayer circles is a full-time job." He laughed, then caught himself. "Actually, I've been meaning to thank you."

"For what?"

"For that talk last semester. You told me faith isn't supposed to fit perfectly, that wrestling with it is what keeps it real. I didn't get it back then, but… I do now."

I blinked. "You remembered that?"

He shrugged, smiling. "Hard to forget when it keeps you from losing your mind."

He looked older somehow, not in age, but in steadiness. The faint shimmer of his card glowed behind his ribs: The Hierophant, upright. Its light was soft, not blinding. Balanced.

"Guess you figured out your own sermon," I said.

He chuckled. "Maybe. But I wouldn't have started without you."

There wasn't much else to say, so I just nodded. He clapped me on the shoulder before leaving, and when he stepped into the sunlight, I felt something loosen in me, like the sound of an old wound unclenching.

I found Grant later that afternoon. He was sitting on a bench outside the philosophy building, notebook open, sunlight glinting off his pen. His sling was gone, though his movements were still careful. The air smelled faintly of chalk and autumn.

"Mind if I join you?" I asked.

He looked up and smiled; tired, but real. "It's your campus too."

I sat beside him. For a while, neither of us spoke. The courtyard buzzed with the low hum of students crossing from one class to the next.

"How's the arm?" I asked finally.

"Better," he said. "Mostly healed." He flexed his fingers once, testing them. "They say I got lucky."

"Oh?"

He closed his notebook. "I wanted to thank you. For checking in after it happened."

I shook my head. "You don't owe me thanks."

"Maybe not," he said. "But I owe you honesty."

That caught me off guard.

He hesitated, then said, "I thought about what Victor said, what I did. I don't blame him anymore. Or you."

I turned toward him. "You don't?"

"No. I blamed everyone for a while. Then I realized… I was the one who chose to listen. He just permitted me to do what I already wanted."

I stared at the stone path beneath our feet. “He told you to cut the rope.”

Grant nodded. “And I did. Just not the way I should’ve.”

The faint shimmer of The Fool flickered in his chest; upright now, its light clear and steady.

“Maybe cutting the rope wasn’t wrong,” I said quietly. “Just... not the time.”

He smiled. “Maybe. Either way, I’m still here.”

“Yeah.”

He stood, stretching his arm gingerly. “You know, he was worried about you.”

I blinked. “Who?”

“Victor. Said he hoped you’d stop seeing him as the enemy.”

The words hit harder than I wanted them to. “He said that?”

“Yeah.” Grant adjusted his bag, slinging it over his shoulder. “He’s not a bad guy, Travis. Just different. You both are.”

He started to walk away, but paused halfway across the courtyard. “For what it’s worth,” he said, “I’m glad you’re both still standing.”

That night, the library was nearly empty. The lamps glowed warm against the dark windows, reflecting our faces like ghosts. Serena was in our usual corner, sketchbook open, sleeves rolled up to her elbows. She didn't look up when I sat down.

"You've been quiet lately," she said.

"Trying it out."

"Does it suit you?"

"Not really."

That made her smile, small and soft.

I leaned back in my chair, watching the rain trace slow paths down the glass. "I saw Nate this morning."

"Oh?"

"He led the service. He was incredible."

"That's good," she said. "He needed something to anchor him."

"I think he found it." I hesitated. "Grant, too. He's doing better."

Her pencil stilled. "You talked to him?"

"Yeah. We made peace."

She closed her book gently, folding her hands on top. "That's something, Travis."

"Feels like the first good something in a while."

Outside, thunder rumbled faintly, though the rain was too light to notice.

After a moment, I said, "I want to make things right with Victor."

Her eyes lifted slowly. "You what?"

"I owe him an apology. Maybe more."

She leaned forward. "You think he'll want to hear it?"

"I don't know."

"Then why do it?"

I looked down at my hands. "Because if I don't, then everything I've learned means nothing. I can't preach about forgiveness and then stay a coward."

Serena was silent for a moment, observing me carefully. Then she said, "You've changed."

"Maybe."

"No," she said softly. "You have. You sound like Elias."

That hit something deep. "He'd tell me I was still doing it wrong."

She smiled faintly. "Probably."

We sat quietly for a while, the rain soft against the window, the smell of old paper filling the room. Then she reached across the table and touched my hand. "If you're going to do this, let me help."

"Serena—"

"No arguments. I want to see how this story ends, too."

I chuckled. "Since when did you start believing in stories?"

"Since one almost killed us."

Later that night, the rain stopped.

I walked back through the courtyard alone. The chapel bell struck nine, echoing across the campus. The grass glittered faintly in the lamplight, and everything smelled clean again.

I passed by the reflection in the library window and, for the first time in months, didn't flinch. The red glow in my chest had dulled to a quiet pulse. The card still burned there, but it didn't feel like a curse anymore, just a reminder.

Elias's words came back to me, as clear as the wind moving through the leaves:

Death doesn't take. It returns.

Maybe that's what this was: a return. Renewal. Judgement without punishment.

The next morning, I'd start with Victor. But for now, I let myself breathe. The night was still. The lamps hummed softly. And for the first time in a long while, the silence didn't scare me. It just sounded like waiting.

Chapter 13: The Lovers

"Upright, union binds... reversed, union breaks."

Sleep didn't come easily anymore. It never did after the Tower. Or after the confrontation with Victor. Every time I closed my eyes, I expected the red light to flare again; to feel the weight of what had been taken and what was left behind.

But that night, exhaustion finally won.

I didn't dream.

At least, not at first.

When I opened my eyes, I was standing in a room that wasn't mine.

The floor was black marble veined with silver, polished so clean it reflected the ceiling, or what I thought was a ceiling until I realized it moved. Stars swam through it. Slow, deliberate, like fish behind glass. There was no sound except the soft, rhythmic ticking of something unseen.

It wasn't a clock. It was slower than that. Older.

The air smelled faintly of rain and iron.

Then a voice spoke, smooth as ink: "Mr. Calder."

I turned.

He stood a few paces away; tall, slender, dressed in a three-piece suit the color of shadow just before dawn. His hair was dark and neat, his eyes gray with the faintest ripple of blue, like storm light reflected in glass.

He held a silver pocket watch, its chain glinting faintly as he turned it once between his fingers.

“Apologies for the intrusion,” he said, calm and deliberate. “Dreams are rarely convenient places to host a guest, but necessity outranks manners. Also, it has been quite some time since I have taken such a form.”

I swallowed. “You’re—”

“Nightmare,” he said, with a polite inclination of the head. “Among other titles. That name will do.”

I took a step back. “You’re real.”

“Reality,” he said, “is a matter of arrangement.”

He smiled faintly, and the air bent with it; not cruel, just wrong, as if the room leaned subtly toward him.

He gestured to a long table that hadn’t been there a moment before: obsidian surface, two chairs.

“Sit,” he said. “You’ll find it easier to think that way.”

I hesitated, then sat. The chair was colder than I thought it should've been.

Nightmare sat across from me, crossing one leg over the other, pocket watch ticking faintly in his hand.

"You've got questions," he said. "And I find I prefer curiosity over fear. It makes the conversation more civilized."

"What is this place?" I asked.

He glanced upward. "The space between. Not quite dream, not quite memory. Think of it as the room where truths wait to be remembered."

The stars above shifted, forming slow-moving constellations that almost looked familiar. Almost.

"You brought me here," I said.

"I invited you," he corrected gently. "You accepted when you slept. When your desire to know overcame the desire to fight."

"Why?"

"Because it's time we talked about what you are, and are not. Perhaps even what you will be." He leaned forward slightly, hands clasped. "You've spent so long staring at the weave, you've mistaken the pattern for the fabric itself."

I frowned. "The cards are the weave."

"They are a weave," he said. "Not the weave. They're lenses; simplified, symbolic. Convenient, but not complete. Some truths cannot be framed by archetypes, Travis. Not even Death."

The word trembled through the air like a bell.

"You speak as though they're alive," I said.

"They are. Every belief that endures long enough learns how to live. But their lives are bound by perception. The cards exist because humans require order. I, on the other hand..." He smiled again. "I exist because order requires shadow."

I stared at him. "You're saying you're not one of them."

"Do I look like art to you?" he asked, amused. "No. I was never painted. I am what spills through the cracks when the symbols fail. The breath between meaning and silence."

The slow, deliberate, certain way he spoke made me feel like he was explaining something I already knew and had just forgotten.

He placed the pocket watch on the table between us. It ticked soundlessly.

"You want to know why your card burns red."

I nodded.

"Because Death was never meant to live in flesh," he said simply. "The arcana are conduits: pure, abstract. When Elias tethered it to you, he forced the infinite into the finite. You became the seam. The point where endings can speak."

My mouth felt dry. "Then what am I now?"

"Both." He tilted his head slightly. "You are the messenger and the message. The one who dies, and the one who returns to tell what it meant."

"Is that a blessing or a curse?"

His smile widened. "Yes."

I gritted my teeth. "You took Elias."

"I reclaimed what was promised," Nightmare said, his tone neither defensive nor cruel. "He offered years that were not his to give. I merely balanced the equation."

"He was trying to protect me."

"As he always did," Nightmare said softly. "A noble act, if futile. You cannot save a flame by hiding it from the wind. You only teach it how to suffocate."

For a moment, silence stretched between us. The ticking grew slower, heavier.

"You hate me for taking him," he said.

I said nothing.

"That's all right," he continued, almost kindly. "Hatred is still a form of acknowledgment. And acknowledgment, for my kind, is worship."

"Don't flatter yourself," I said.

He laughed; not loud, but genuine. "Ah, there he is. The boy Elias was saved. Still pretending the universe is a moral debate."

I stood. "What do you want from me?"

"Nothing," he said, rising as well. "What I offer you, however, is understanding."

He paced slowly, hands behind his back.

"The deck you see, the cards in every living chest, is an interpretation of consequence. But consequence is not truth. The truth is that every life bends the weave, and every death rewrites it. You, Travis Calder, have become the hinge. You can step outside the pattern."

"I didn't ask for that."

"No one ever does," he said simply.

The stars above us shifted again, one falling slow and long across the black. Its reflection rippled across the marble floor.

"What happens if I step outside it?" I asked.

Nightmare's gaze sharpened, the faintest thrill of something like amusement in his tone. "Then you stop being predictable. The cards no longer dictate your meaning. You write your own."

He leaned closer, voice almost whispering.

"But beware. The moment you begin to write, the deck will write back."

The watch between us ticked once, loud enough to crack the silence.

"What are you telling me?" I asked.

"That the game has changed," he said softly. "The weave is unraveling, Travis. Something stirs beneath the pattern, something even I did not summon."

"What does that mean?"

He looked past me, as if watching something distant and invisible move. "It means the deck is waking. And when it does, you'll need to decide whether you're part of its dream… or its dreamer."

The air trembled.

"Why tell me this?"

"Because," he said, stepping back into the dark, "you and I share a thread now. When the weave breaks, you'll understand which side you've been standing on."

The light dimmed. The ticking stopped. The stars overhead began to fade, swallowed by an unseen tide. Nightmare's voice came once more, faint, distant, polite as ever:

"Sleep well, Mr. Calder. Morning always believes it's the first to arrive. And do not fret, you have time to decide."

I woke to sunlight through the dorm window, cold sweat clinging to my skin.

The room was quiet, the world unchanged.

But when I looked down, the card in my chest pulsed once: not red, but white.

And momentarily, I swore I could hear a clock ticking beneath my heartbeat.

Chapter 14: Wheel of Fortune

"Upright, fate turns forward... reversed, fate turns against."

Serena and I met Lena in the student café near the music hall, which always smelled like cinnamon and wet paper. Lena sat by the window, her hair pulled back, notes spread like a miniature courtroom. When she saw us, her eyes narrowed just enough to make me reconsider coming.

"Travis Calder," she said, like it was a warning.

"Lena," I said, trying to smile. "Can we talk?"

"You can," she said dryly, "but whether I listen depends on what comes next."

Serena sat beside me. "It's important," she said softly.

Lena sighed and leaned back. "You want to talk about Victor."

I nodded.

She studied me like she was measuring the distance between past and apology. "I heard you've been quiet lately," she said. "David says you've changed."

"Maybe," I said. "Or maybe I finally understand what I broke."

Her expression softened a little. "You mean Grant."

"And Victor," I said. "I want to make things right."

Lena tilted her head. “And why now?”

“Because I think I was wrong about everything.”

She didn’t say anything for a moment. The hall’s hum filled the space between us: low voices, shuffling footsteps, the faint hiss of the instrumental harmony. Finally, she folded her notes closed. “You hurt him, Travis. Not just once. You made him doubt himself when he was trying to help. He won’t want to see you.”

“I know,” I said. “But I need to try.”

Serena reached across the table, her hand brushing mine, grounding me. “Please,” she said. “For both of them.”

Lena exhaled, the sound sharp and tired. “He’s not angry, just closed off,” she said. “But he listens when I talk.” She looked at me. “If I arrange it, you don’t get to justify what you did. You just listen.”

“I will,” I said. “That’s all I want.”

Lena’s eyes lingered on me for a heartbeat, then she nodded. “The chapel. Tomorrow night. He still practices there sometimes, the piano, not prayers.” She gathered her notes. “Don’t make me regret this.”

When she left, Serena leaned back, relief softening her features. "You handled that better than I thought."

"Progress," I said.

"Or a calm before another storm."

The next evening, the chapel was nearly empty. The doors creaked when I pushed them open. Candles lined the altar, thin flames trembling like they were afraid to be seen. The air smelled faintly of dust and old hymns.

Victor sat at the piano near the front, his back to me. He wasn't playing; his fingers hovered over the keys like trying to remember a melody he'd forgotten halfway through.

He didn't turn when I stepped closer. "Lena said you'd come," he said.

"I wanted to talk."

"I figured." He pressed one key, a low note that echoed through the space. "You brought a friend?"

"Just me."

He nodded, then stood slowly. When he faced me, I saw how tired he looked; not sickly, just older in some quiet, internal way.

"What do you want, Travis?"

The question wasn't sharp. It was weary. Tired of the games I played with him, but he was never a player; just a crooked picture in the hall of what should've been perfection from the old man's eyes.

"I came to say I'm sorry," I said. "For what happened. For what I thought you were."

He crossed his arms. "You thought I was evil."

"I thought you were dangerous," I corrected. "And I let someone else's fear tell me what to see."

He studied me for a long moment. Then he said, "You weren't entirely wrong."

I frowned. "What do you mean?"

He gestured around the chapel. "This place, all of it, was built on the idea that meaning comes from above. That there's a pattern we can't escape. But I've never believed that." He paused. "Maybe that makes me dangerous to people who do."

"That's not—" I started, then stopped. "You don't believe in G-d?"

"I don't believe in fate," he said simply. "Not the kind that forgives itself by calling suffering destiny."

The candlelight flickered. He walked toward the altar, tracing his fingers along the edge. "People need symbols, Travis. They need stories that tell them their pain has a purpose. I used to envy that." He glanced back at me. "Until I saw how much harm it can do."

"You mean Grant."

He nodded. "I told him to leave his mother. I meant it as mercy. He took it as permission. Belief did the rest."

I swallowed hard. "It wasn't your fault."

He smiled faintly. "Maybe not. But neither was it fate. That's the danger of faith: it forgives the accidents of our cruelty."

I let the words settle between us. For once, I didn't argue.

After a moment, I said, "I talked to something. Something that said the cards are just lenses. That we're the ones who give them power."

He raised an eyebrow. "You talked to something?"

I nodded. "Nightmare. The thing Elias, my mentor, made the bargain with. It's... a long story."

Victor exhaled through his nose, belief and surprise in one motion. "And what did it say?"

"That the weave is unraveling. That belief makes it hold. That the cards don't rule us; we rule them."

He gave a quiet laugh. "So you've found philosophy in your demons."

"Maybe," I said. "But if belief is what binds everything, then maybe disbelief is what can free us."

He turned, facing me fully now. "That's a dangerous idea."

"I know."

For a while, neither of us spoke. The snow outside had started, soft against the stained glass.

Finally, he said, "You want to make things right?"

"Yes."

"Then stop looking for patterns," he said. "Start looking for choices."

Its simplicity hit harder than any lecture Elias ever gave me. I nodded slowly. "I'll try."

"Good," he said, his voice softening. "Because, for what it's worth, I'm sorry too. You were trying to make sense of something that isn't meant to make sense. That kind of confusion can make anyone cruel."

He extended a hand.

I took it. His palm was warm, steady.

The air between us didn't feel poisoned for the first time since Grant's accident.

When I stepped outside, Serena was waiting by the chapel gate, dressed in a coat and scarf. “So?” she asked.

“It went better than I deserved.”

She smiled faintly. “That's usually the best kind of ending.”

We walked through the empty courtyard, the snow light enough to feel like a child's blessing. I told her about Victor, his disbelief, and his choice words. She listened, quiet as the world around us.

“You think he's right?” she asked finally.

“I think belief is a mirror,” I said. “It shows what we already expect to see. Maybe that's why I saw monsters in the dark.”

“And what do you see now?”

I looked up. The clouds had thinned, revealing the moon's faint glow above the chapel spire. “Possibility,” I said. “And maybe something worth fixing.”

She looked at me sidelong. “You mean us.”

“Among other things.”

She nudged me gently with her elbow. “You’re planning something.”

“Not a plan,” I said. “A start. I want to make up for what I did, not just to Victor, but to everything I believed without question.”

“That sounds like a plan.”

“Then maybe it is.”

The snow fell gently. For the first time, it didn’t feel like a warning. It felt like a beginning.

Later that night, I sat by my window, watching the snowflakes trace their way down the sky. The world felt smaller, but clearer somehow.

The card in my chest pulsed once in the reflection: faint, blue this time, not red.

Not Death.

Change.

And somewhere far away, beneath the whisper of snow, I thought I heard a quiet ticking again:patient, measured, waiting for what came next.

Chapter 15: The Empress

"Upright, creation overwhelms... reversed, creation withers."

The snow didn't stop for three days.

When the trains started running again, Havenbrook was half-buried beneath white, and the world had gone silent. The chapel bells still rang, faint and far away, but their sound was muffled, like the snow had swallowed even the idea of sound itself.

Serena and I stood on the platform with our luggage and matching exhaustion, scarves wound too tightly around our necks, watching our breath fog into the frozen air. She glanced at me once, her eyes bright and steady in the morning light.

"You sure about this?" she asked.

"Going home?"

She nodded. "It's been... a long semester."

"Yeah," I said. "That's the point."

The train arrived with a metallic groan, doors opening to a gust of heat and oil-scented air. We boarded wordlessly, sliding into a pair of seats by the window. The countryside blurred by in shades of gray and white: frozen rivers, distant roofs, forests turned skeletal in winter.

For a while, neither of us spoke. I watched her reflection in the window, her face half in shadow and half in light, and thought how strange it felt to see her outside Havenbrook, as if we were leaving one world and entering another.

"How long has it been since you saw them?" she asked softly.

"Almost a year. I went with David for summer vacation."

She smiled faintly. "They'll be happy to have you back."

"Maybe," I said. "They never knew how much had changed."

"They don't need to," she said. "You're their son. That's enough."

Her voice carried the quiet certainty I always envied, like faith, but not the kind that required proof. I let the train rhythm fill the silence between us, the steady clatter on rails like a heartbeat. The snow fell heavily outside, swallowing the world one flake at a time.

My family's house stood at the end of a cul-de-sac, brick and old enough to creak in the wind. A small wreath hung crooked on the door, and smoke curled faintly from the chimney. It looked the same; like no time had passed, like I hadn't died once and come back carrying a red light in my chest.

The door opened before I could knock.

"Travis," my mother said, her voice catching between surprise and relief. Then she hugged me, fiercely, as if she could still feel the boy who used to fit under her chin. The smell of cinnamon and laundry soap filled my lungs, childhood and forgiveness in one breath.

When she pulled back, her eyes found Serena. "And this must be the friend I've heard about."

Serena smiled, polite but warm. "Thank you for letting me visit."

"Visit?" my mother said. "Nonsense. You're family for as long as you're under this roof."

Then she winked at me. "You always did have good taste."

"Mom—"

"What? I'm old, not blind."

I could feel my face heat as Serena laughed softly behind me.

My younger brother, Noah, thundered down the stairs. "Travis! You're back!" He skidded across the floor in socks, nearly colliding with the wall, then flung himself into a hug that almost knocked the wind out of me. He'd grown taller, almost my height now, but still carried a faint scent of pencil shavings and bubblegum.

My sister, Clara, followed more gracefully, waving from behind a mug of hot chocolate. “Welcome home, prodigal son.”

“I’m not the prodigal one,” I said.

“You disappeared for a year and wrote two emails.” She grinned. “Definitely the prodigal one.”

Serena laughed again, and for the first time in months, the sound didn’t feel like something fragile.

Dinner that night was a kind of organized chaos only my family could manage. My father, still in his office clothes, was balancing a phone call and a pot roast. My mother was simultaneously chopping vegetables, giving instructions, and telling Clara to stop interrogating Serena about her “mysterious art major friend group.”

“I’m in theology,” Serena said, smiling.

“Oh!” Clara said, eyes bright. “So like, exorcisms?”

Serena raised an eyebrow. “Not the kind you’re imagining.”

David would’ve loved that, I thought, a houseful of noise and jokes and people who didn’t care about fate or patterns.

My father finally hung up the phone and turned, grinning. “Travis. Still keeping your nose clean?”

“Trying.”

He clapped a hand on my shoulder. "That's my boy. Serena, do you eat meat?"

"I eat everything," she said, and my mother laughed.

By the time the table was set, it looked like a feast. After the prayer, the sound of forks filled the room, the hum of stories being told simultaneously. Noah talked about his school projects. Clara announced she'd passed her driving test on the second try. My mother told a story about when Dad accidentally sent his boss an email full of bad puns. Serena added her own tales from Havenbrook: the eccentric professors, the mystic theory debates, the endless cups of bad coffee.

I mainly stayed quiet, watching them all. The light from the chandelier turned everything gold. For once, I wasn't thinking about cards or destinies or bargains. I watched my family laugh, and Serena laughed with them.

My mom caught my gaze and mouthed, *She's lovely.*

I nodded in agreement.

After dinner, the house quieted. My dad built a fire in the living room, the wood popping as the flames took hold. Serena sat curled on the couch, tea in hand, eyes tracing the firelight. My mother asked her about her studies, my father teased me about "finally bringing home someone smarter," and Noah fell asleep halfway through a movie he insisted we watch.

The world felt small again, safe. It wasn't something I'd realized I missed until that moment: the ordinary noise of people who didn't know what it meant to die and come back changed.

Serena and I stayed by the fire when my parents finally went upstairs.

"You have a good family," she said softly.

"Yeah," I said. "I forget that sometimes."

"Why?"

"Because it's easier to think I came from nowhere. Makes the rest of it hurt less."

She tilted her head, studying me. "You still think you were chosen for something?"

"I think I was cursed with meaning," I said. "It's different."

She smiled faintly. "You're still here, Travis. That means something too."

I didn't answer. I didn't need to.

The fire crackled, painting her face in shifting amber. For a moment, she looked like she belonged entirely to another world, untouched by cards or fate.

When the flames dimmed, we went upstairs. My room was exactly as I'd left it: posters, stacks of books, the faint smell of dust and ink. Serena stood by the window, watching snow fall under the streetlight.

"You okay?" she asked.

"Yeah," I said. "It's strange. I expected to feel… haunted here."

"And do you?"

I shook my head. "No. Not even a little."

She smiled softly. "Good."

She reached out, brushing her fingers along my desk, the same one I'd studied at as a kid. "You kept everything."

"I guess I didn't know what else to do with it."

Her hand lingered on a photo frame; my family was at the lake years ago, before everything changed. "You look happy here," she said.

"I was."

The silence that followed wasn't awkward. It was soft, tentative, like something was waiting to be said.

"I've been meaning to ask you something," I said finally.

Serena turned, leaning against the window frame. "That sounds serious."

"It's not," I lied. Then, after a beat: "Actually, it is."

Her eyes softened. "Okay."

I took a breath. "After everything we've seen, Elias, Nightmare, Victor, I realized something. I've spent years trying to read meaning into everything. Every shadow, every sign, every word. But maybe the point isn't to understand. Maybe it's to feel."

She tilted her head, a small smile curving her lips. "You sound like Elias when you say that."

"Then I've learned something."

She laughed, quiet and warm.

"I guess what I'm trying to say," I continued, "is that I don't want to analyze what this is." I gestured between us. "I just want to be in it. If you'll let me."

Her smile faltered, not from doubt, but from something gentler. She stepped closer. "You're asking me?"

I nodded. "No cards, no omens. Just me."

Her hand brushed my chest, where the card pulsed faintly beneath my shirt. "Not even that?"

"For once," I said, "I don't care what it says."

She looked at me a moment longer, then kissed me.

It wasn't a hesitant kiss. It was quiet, sure, the kind that said we made it this far. Her hand slid to my cheek, my breath catching in the cold air between us.

When we finally broke apart, she rested her forehead against mine.

"You know," she whispered, "for someone haunted by Death, you're bad at letting things end."

"Good," I said. "I'd rather start something."

She laughed softly, and it filled the room with light.

We lay there after, just talking about everything and nothing. She told me about the first time she saw me in class, hunched over my notes like the world depended on it. I told her how Elias used to say love was a "dangerous form of magic."

Outside, snow kept falling, thick and steady. The sound was like breathing.

When she finally fell asleep beside me, I stared at the ceiling, the faint glow of the card flickering under my ribs. It wasn't red anymore. Not burning. It pulsed blue: calm, slow, alive.

For the first time, I didn't see it as a curse.

Maybe Elias had been wrong all along.

Maybe the cards didn't dictate who we were; they only reflected what we believed ourselves to be. And maybe, just possibly, belief could change.

I glanced at Serena, her head resting lightly against my shoulder, her breath steady and soft.

Outside, the world was white, clean, beginning again.

And for the first time in months, I didn't feel Death's shadow at my back.

I didn't feel chosen. I didn't feel cursed. I just felt alive.

If Death had brought me back to learn anything, it was this: the cards could show fates and choices, lives and losses, but they couldn't measure love, the small, human kind that held the world together without magic.

And that night, as snow buried the streets in silence, I fell asleep without fear for the first time since the accident. Not because the cards were silent. But because I no longer needed them to speak.

Chapter 16: The Fool

"Upright, the abyss calls... reversed, the abyss consumes."

The train from my hometown rolled into Havenbrook under a pale winter sun, cutting through the frost like a dull blade. The snow had finally started to melt, leaving slush pooling between the courtyard bricks. Even the statues that guarded the college gates looked weary of winter.

By the time Serena and I reached Crown Café, the morning crowd had already claimed every table. Students leaned over steaming cups, half-listening to each other, half-dreaming about spring. The bell above the door chimed when we stepped in, a slight sound swallowed by chatter and espresso hiss.

"Feels smaller," Serena said, pulling off her gloves.

"Maybe we got taller," I said.

"You didn't."

I smiled, bumping her shoulder lightly. The warmth hit us like memories: roasted coffee, syrup, cinnamon. It was the smell of mornings before everything had changed drastically, before towers, demons, and death cards.

David was already there, waving us over from the usual corner by the ivy window. Maya sat across from him, hair tucked under a green beanie, sketching something on the sleeve of a napkin. The moment she looked up, her eyes widened.

"Finally!" she shouted, drawing curious stares from nearby tables. "The prodigals return!"

"Keep your voice down," David muttered. "You're scaring the caffeine addicts."

Maya ignored him, grinning at us. "You two look disgustingly happy. Did you get possessed by optimism over break?"

Serena slid into the seat beside her, laughing. "Something like that."

David gave me a suspicious look. "You're smiling. That's usually a bad omen."

I sat down. "Maybe I'm trying something new."

"Oh no," Maya said, eyes narrowing. "You're both glowing. You're together, aren't you?"

The words hung between us, sharp but playful. Serena didn't deny it. She just reached for my hand across the table; casual, but not careless.

Eli's mouth dropped open. "Wait. Seriously? Since when?"

"Since winter break," I said.

He blinked. "I leave you two alone for two weeks, and this happens. I should've known. There was foreshadowing."

Maya clapped her hands together. "Finally! The tension was unbearable. Do you know how many people were betting on when you figured it out?"

I frowned. "People were betting?"

"Oh, absolutely," she said. "I made twenty bucks off Serena last semester."

"You bet against me?" Serena asked.

Maya grinned. "I bet on dramatic timing. You didn't disappoint."

David leaned back, smirking. "So, the Oracle of Havenbrook found something other than omens to obsess over. Proud of you, man."

"Thanks," I said dryly.

The waitress appeared with a tray, already knowing our orders. She didn't ask how; she'd seen this group enough times to predict our patterns. Maya's monstrosity of a triple-shot latte, Eli's black coffee, Serena's herbal tea, and my cocoa.

Maya raised her cup. "To new beginnings!"

We clinked mugs, laughter echoing softly against the window glass.

For a while, it felt like nothing bad had ever happened here, just friends, caffeine, and the illusion of peace.

Serena pulled out a small stack of folded notes, spreading them across the table. "So. I was thinking of our next semester schedules."

David groaned. "We just got back."

"Exactly," she said. "Which means we can still fix your bad decisions."

"I only took one philosophy elective," he said.

"Metaphysics and Consequence?"

"It sounded cool!"

"Professor Greaves teaches it. He's the one who believes gravity is a moral illusion."

"Still sounds cool."

Maya sipped her drink. "You're both nerds."

"You draw skeletons kissing angels," David shot back.

"That's art."

"It's therapy."

They bickered, easy and familiar. I let them fill the silence, my hand still loosely in Serena's. Through the window, the morning light had shifted from silver to gold, cutting through the ivy in fractured shapes.

It was almost normal. Almost.

And yet, beneath it, I felt something different. A faint hum under my ribs, where the card slept. Not red this time, not angry, just... restless. Like it was listening.

Serena caught my expression. "You okay?"

"Yeah," I said. "Just thinking."

"About?"

"Nothing worth ruining breakfast over."

She studied me briefly, then nodded, the kind of understanding you earn after months of shared silence.

Maya stretched, kicking David under the table. "So, what's next, Oracle? Are you planning to retire now that you've found true love, or will you still freak out whenever someone mentions destiny?"

"I'm taking a break," I said.

"From destiny?"

"From seeing patterns where there aren't any."

"Good luck with that," David said. "You can't even order coffee without reading into it."

"That's a fair critique."

Serena smiled faintly. "He's trying."

"Trying's a start," Maya said. "Just don't turn into one of those guys who start every sentence with 'My girlfriend and I.'"

I grinned. "Wouldn't dream of it."

The café door opened again, the bell chiming softly. A gust of cold air swept in, carrying the smell of snow and iron. I didn't look up immediately until the noise at our table stilled.

Victor Morrell stood at the entrance.

He was out of his uniform, wearing a dark coat and gloves, a thin line of frost in his hair. He scanned the room once, then found us. The look he gave wasn't hostile, just deliberate.

"Speak of the devil," David muttered.

Maya elbowed him. "Don't jinx it."

Victor crossed the café, his steps quiet but confident. The conversations around us dimmed in that instinctive way crowds react to someone who doesn't quite belong to the noise.

He stopped at our table. "Travis."

"Victor."

He nodded to Serena, to the others. "May I?"

David looked at me. "Should I get a crucifix or something?"

"Please don't," Serena whispered.

Victor ignored him. His gaze held mine. "I'd like a word. In private."

Maya arched an eyebrow. "That's not ominous at all."

I hesitated. His voice had no hostility, just a strange weight, like he'd been carrying the sentence for days.

Serena's hand tightened around mine. "You don't have to."

"I know," I said. "But I think I should."

Victor inclined his head slightly, almost polite. "The roof of the philosophy hall," he said. "When you're ready."

Then he turned and left, the bell chiming again as the door shut.

The silence that followed was heavier than it should've been.

Maya finally exhaled. "Okay, someone tell me we're not about to get another exorcism arc."

"Probably not," Serena said, though her voice lacked conviction.

David leaned forward, elbows on the table. "You sure about this?"

"No," I admitted. "But he sounded… different."

"Different how?"

"Like he's figured something out. Or maybe like he's scared."

Serena frowned. "Victor doesn't scare easily."

"Exactly."

Maya sipped her coffee, eyes narrowing. "You're going, aren't you?"

"I have to," I said. "Whatever this is, it's connected. I can feel it."

David sighed. "Of course you can."

Serena touched my arm. "I'll come with you."

I shook my head. "Not this time. He asked for me."

Her jaw tightened, but she didn't argue. "Fine. But I'm calling campus security if you're not back in an hour."

"Fair."

Maya grinned weakly. “Should we start praying or something?”

“Maybe just keep my cocoa warm.”

She raised her mug in mock salute. “Consider it done.”

Outside, the courtyard had quieted again. The snow had stopped falling, but the air carried that electric stillness that comes after. The path to the philosophy hall was half-frozen, my boots crunching through the thin ice crust.

As I walked, the faint hum under my ribs returned, the pulse of the card, steady and calm, but listening.

I remembered Nightmare’s words, echoing in sleep and silence alike:

There is a space between the weavings, and I exist because of disbelief. Through disbelief, you can pass beyond the weave.

Whatever that meant, I felt Victor knew more than he should.

And maybe, for the first time, I wasn’t afraid to find out.

Chapter 17: Chariot

"Upright, victory through will... reversed, defeat through chaos."

The philosophy hall always felt like it belonged to another century. Its spire leaned a little, as if even stone could grow tired of holding too much thought. The lamps along the path buzzed faintly, a low hum that bled into the cold air.

By the time I reached the door, the courtyard was empty. Most students had fled indoors for warmth. The sky was bruised purple, the kind of evening that looks like it's been holding its breath too long.

I climbed the narrow stairs, each one groaning underfoot. My hand brushed the rail, slick with frost. When I pushed open the roof door, the wind greeted me: sharp, clean, unkind.

Victor stood there, face almost as cold as the air at first.

He stood near the edge, his back to me, coat flaring slightly in the wind. His breath fogged the air. The last of the daylight washed him in gray-blue, outlining him against the horizon.

For a moment, he didn't move. Then he said, "You came."

"I said I would."

He turned, hands in his pockets, expression unreadable. "You've changed."

"People keep saying that."

"They're right," he said quietly. "You used to look like someone searching for a map. Now you look like someone who's already seen where it leads."

"Not sure that's an improvement."

Victor smiled faintly; not mockery, not kindness, just understanding. "Sometimes clarity hurts more than ignorance."

The wind caught between us, pulling his words apart. I stepped closer. "You said you wanted to talk."

He nodded, looking out again over the courtyard. "Do you ever think about what he said to you?"

"Who?"

"The demon."

My pulse quickened. "Nightmare."

He nodded once. "That's the one. You told me, he said, there's a space between the weavings."

"Yes."

Victor tilted his head. "Do you know what that means?"

"I was hoping you did."

He gave a low laugh, dry and self-aware. "You always assume I have the answers."

"I assume you've thought about them more than I have."

"That's fair," he admitted. "But thinking doesn't always mean understanding. Sometimes it just means spinning in circles until the floor disappears."

He turned back toward me. "Still, I've been considering what he said. The weavings, the cards, the patterns, whatever you call them, are not laws. They are structure. They define possibility, not certainty. What Nightmare described sounds like what exists outside that structure."

"Beyond fate," I said.

"Exactly. The space between meanings. Between what's possible and what's believed."

I frowned. "Then why say he exists because of disbelief?"

"Because disbelief is the only way to see beyond structure," he said simply. "Faith binds. Doubt breaks. If everyone believes the world is woven in one way, that pattern becomes law. Disbelief creates the gaps."

I let that sink in. The wind scraped against the rooftop, cold against my face. "So… he's real because people stop believing?"

"Or because they start questioning what belief even means."

"That's not comforting."

"It's not meant to be," Victor said. "He's not a savior. He's a consequence."

I looked down at my hands, remembering the red light that had once burned there. "Then what am I?"

Victor didn't answer right away. He walked to the edge, staring down at the courtyard below. "You're the bridge," he said finally. "The one who stands between faith and disbelief. Death, but also return. You carry both meanings; the card and what lies beyond it."

"I didn't ask for that."

"Neither did anyone who ever mattered."

I gave a short, humorless laugh. "You're starting to sound like Elias."

Victor's jaw tightened slightly, and for a moment the air went still. "He sounded like he was a good man," he said. "But he built his faith on walls. You can't protect truth by locking it away."

"He tried," I said softly. "And it killed him."

Victor's gaze softened. "Then maybe the lesson is that truth doesn't want to be protected."

I turned toward the horizon. The sun had finally vanished, leaving only the afterlight, a faint orange bleeding into gray. "You didn't bring me up here to talk philosophy."

"Didn't I?"

"Not just that," I said. "You said you had something to show me."

He hesitated, then reached into his coat pocket. When his hand came out, he was holding a small object; not a card, but a thin strip of parchment, folded several times over.

"I found this," he said, offering it. "In the Havenbrook archives."

I took it carefully. The parchment was brittle, old enough to crumble if mishandled. In the dim light, I could just make out faint, circular markings, as if part sigil, part diagram.

"What is it?"

"Notes," Victor said. "Elias's, signed by him. Or something older that he modified. It mentions a 'point of unraveling' where the weave grows thin. A threshold between belief and void."

I looked up. "You think Nightmare came from there."

"I think everything that doesn't fit came from there," he said. "Ghosts, myths, even cards. They're all echoes of the space between. If he exists because of disbelief, then that place, whatever it is, might be what happens when the world stops believing entirely."

My chest tightened. "And you want to find it."

He nodded. "We need to."

"Why?"

He hesitated, eyes flicking to the horizon again. "Because it's classic, textbook, apocalypse. A weaving, a space between, and the between consumes the reality. Nightmare is not just a byproduct. He's a herald."

The word felt like it carried weight, but it shouldn't. "You think he's trying to break the world."

Victor shook his head slowly. "No. I think he's showing us how fragile it already is."

We stood in silence for a long moment. Below us, the lamps flickered on across the courtyard, one by one, small stars fighting the dusk.

Finally, I said, "It doesn't make sense, though? Why would he then offer me to join him?"

Victor didn't answer immediately. The wind filled the pause, carrying the low groan of the building beneath us. He turned the parchment over in his hands, eyes unfocused, as though the answer might be written somewhere between the folds.

"Maybe," he said finally, "because you already have one foot in that space."

I frowned. "What's that supposed to mean?"

"You died once, right?" Victor said simply. "You crossed the threshold and returned carrying what shouldn't have followed you. Nightmare didn't choose you, Travis; he recognized you."

The words hit harder than I wanted them to. I stepped closer to the edge, the courtyard below a shifting blur of lamplight and shadow. "Recognized me as what?"

Victor's voice softened. "A fracture. The place where faith and disbelief meet. The Death card isn't about endings, it's about the space after, right? The in-between."

"So, what?" I asked. "I'm some kind of doorway?"

"Maybe not a doorway," he said. "Maybe a mirror. Nightmares reflect what we refuse to see. He shows you the absence you try to fill with meaning. Maybe that's why he spoke to you."

I exhaled, the air clouding between us. "And he wants me to help him destroy the weave?"

"Or redefine it," Victor said. "You said he called disbelief creation. Maybe what he's offering isn't destruction. Maybe he wants to build something where belief can't dictate the shape of everything."

I turned toward him. "You almost sound like you agree with him."

Victor gave a quiet laugh. "I disagree with demons. But I understand their logic."

"Which is?"

"That creation and chaos share the same roots. Everything we build, we first have to break."

The wind picked up, tugging at our coats. The parchment in his hand fluttered like a living thing.

"Then what happens if the weave breaks completely?" I asked. "If disbelief wins?"

Victor looked out across the rooftops, his expression unreadable. “Then maybe everything ends. Or maybe everything starts over.”

“That’s not comforting.”

He smiled faintly. “It’s not meant to be.”

Silence again. The sky had gone darker, the moon cutting through thin clouds like the edge of a blade. Beneath it, the world seemed smaller, the lights of Havenbrook flickering like stars caught in glass.

I looked at him. “You said we need to find it. This point of unraveling.”

“Yes.”

“Then what? What happens when we stand at the edge of the void?”

He met my gaze. “We decide whether to step in.”

I stared at him, unsure if he was serious. “You really think we’ll find it?”

“I think it’s already finding us.”

There was something in his tone: calm, certain, almost reverent. For the first time, I realized that Victor wasn’t just unafraid of the unknown; he belonged to it. He moved through disbelief like it was air.

And maybe that was what scared me most.

"You sound like Elias," I said again, though my voice came out quieter this time. "When he used to talk about the weave, about how it chose people."

Victor's expression softened. "Maybe he was right. Maybe it did choose. But not for the reasons he thought."

"What reasons, then?"

"To see if we'd ever learn to choose back."

I opened my mouth, but no words came. The wind had gone still again, and the world seemed to hold its breath in that stillness.

Somewhere far off, the chapel bell began to toll. Once. Twice. The sound echoed through the dark like a heartbeat.

Victor turned toward the stairs. "Come on," he said. "It's getting late."

"Wait," I said. "If Nightmare's right… If disbelief is what holds the space between, what happens to people like me? The ones who've seen both sides?"

He paused at the door, hand on the handle. "Then maybe we stop being believers or doubters," he said. "Maybe we become something else."

"What?"

He looked back at me, his silhouette framed against the pale light. "Witnesses."

The door creaked shut behind him, leaving me alone on the roof.

For a long time, I didn't move. The parchment fluttered against my palm, whispering like something alive. The air felt thinner now, the stars sharp enough to cut.

I looked down at the courtyard, the faint shapes of students passing, the faint hum of laughter from the café below, and I wondered which world I was standing in: the one built from faith or crumbling from disbelief.

And then, somewhere between the wind and the silence, I thought I heard it again: a voice like a thread unraveling.

You can't serve both meaning and truth, Travis. One always eats the other.

When I finally went inside, the echo of that voice followed me down the stairs, quiet as breath, constant as gravity.

Chapter 18: Strength

"Upright, courage and grace... reversed, fear and rage."

The snow had begun to fall again by the time we returned to the dorms. The sky hung low, heavy with clouds that never committed to rain or light. It was the kind of evening that made everything sound distant, the echo of footsteps, the sigh of the wind through the chapel eaves, the faint hum of the courtyard lamps.

Serena, who waited at the foot of the philosophy hall, followed me to her dorm room, where we stealthily snuck in. She set her bag down near the heater and rubbed her hands together, her breath still visible in the dim air.

"You've been quiet since the roof," she said.

"I've been thinking."

"That's new," she teased softly.

I sat on the edge of her bed, staring at the fogged-up window. "Victor's serious about this," I said finally. "He thinks we can find it. The space between the weavings. The place Nightmare came from."

Serena sank into the chair across from me, tucking her legs beneath her. "And you want to go with him."

It wasn't a question.

"I think I have to."

She nodded slowly, as if she'd already known that answer, as if she'd been dreading it since the moment she saw the red glow return to my chest. "You don't have to do anything alone, you know. Or at all."

"I'm not doing it alone," I said. "Not this time."

"That's not what I mean." She leaned forward, elbows on her knees. "You keep talking like this is your burden. Like you were chosen for something. But maybe the point of all this, the cards, Elias, even Nightmare, isn't to carry it. Maybe it's time to let it go."

I looked at her. "And if letting go means the world unravels?"

"Then maybe it needs to," she said quietly. "You keep talking about fate like it's a thread you're afraid to drop. But what if strength isn't holding on? What if it's the courage to let it break?"

I didn't answer. The words cut close; too close to what I'd been trying not to think about since the Tower. The image of Elias's face, calm in that final moment, flickered behind my eyes.

"I can't just walk away," I said finally. "Elias died trying to protect me. If I ignore what he started, what he gave up, then it's like it meant nothing."

Serena's voice softened. "Or maybe that's exactly why you should stop. He gave you a life. Not a mission."

I ran a hand through my hair. "If I do nothing, Nightmare keeps feeding on disbelief. He keeps spreading. He's already tied to me; I feel it whenever the air shifts. If we don't stop him—"

"You'll die trying?" she interrupted, her voice sharp now. "You realize that's what this sounds like, right? You and Victor are marching off to face some cosmic nightmare because you think you're the only ones who can. That's not strength, Travis. That's martyrdom."

Her words hung in the air like static. Outside, the snow had started again, gentle but relentless.

I stood, pacing. "You think I want this? You think I want to play savior? I'm terrified, Serena. I half expect not to see myself whenever I look in the mirror. But if I do nothing, if I just wait for someone else to fix this, then Elias really did die for nothing. Then," I whisper, "you may die."

Silence sat between us for a few minutes before Serena's eyes glimmered, not with anger now, but with something more profound. "And what about me? You think I can just watch you walk into something you might not return from?"

I stopped pacing. "That's why I'm telling you now."

"Why?" she asked, her voice trembling. "So, I can prepare to lose you?"

"No," I said, quieter. "So, you know that if I don't make it, it wasn't because I didn't try to return."

She closed her eyes, pressing her hands to her face. For a moment, neither of us moved. The heater clicked softly, the sound too small for what hung between us.

When she finally spoke, her voice was steadier. "You keep talking about strength like it's a sacrifice. But that's not what it is. Strength is choosing to live, even when it's easier to die for something."

I sat beside her. "And if I don't get to choose?"

"You do," she said, meeting my eyes. "You always do."

The silence that followed wasn't empty; it was a space where words couldn't go, where only understanding could exist. I reached for her hand, and she didn't pull away.

After a while, she said, "If you go after Nightmare, promise me one thing."

"Anything. Everything."

"Promise me you'll come back different, not gone."

I smiled faintly. "You realize that's the same thing, right?"

She squeezed my hand. "Then promise anyway."

"I promise Serena."

The wind outside shifted, brushing against the window like a sigh. The faint reflection of the card in my chest glimmered in the glass, no longer red, but a soft gold. Calm. Waiting.

Serena leaned her head against my shoulder. "You're not alone in this," she said. "Not anymore."

"I know."

"You're still scared, though."

"Yeah."

"Good," she said softly. "Keep that. Fear means you still have something to lose."

For a long time, we just sat there, watching the snow thicken against the pane. The world outside looked suspended, quiet, fragile, endless.

Finally, she whispered, "Whatever happens, don't let it define you."

"What if it already has?"

"Then redefine it," she said. "That's what strength really is."

I closed my eyes, breathing in the quiet, the warmth, the steady rhythm of her heartbeat against my arm. "Only we define ourselves," I smile weakly. She smiled and snuggled against me.

Outside, the storm gathered in slow circles, wind tracing invisible patterns through the dark. Somewhere in that pattern, I imagined I could hear Nightmare's voice again, not as a threat, but as an echo.

To stand between faith and disbelief is to stand where G-d fears to look.

Maybe that was what strength meant, not conquering the dark, but refusing to look away from it.

And for the first time, I thought I understood what Elias had seen in me, not a chosen one, not a savior, but a boy who had died once and still dared to live again.

The next morning, I woke before the sun.

The room was still, the kind of quiet that doesn't feel peaceful so much as paused. The radiator clicked once near the wall, and snow pressed faintly against the glass outside the window like it was trying to listen in.

Serena had fallen asleep next to me, one hand tangled in the blanket she'd thrown over us, her breathing even and soft. The lamp on the table was still on, its light spilling across her sketchbook; half-finished lines of something she hadn't had the heart to finish so late.

For a while, I just watched her. I told myself it was to make sure she was there, but the truth was more straightforward: it was the only moment that felt real in days.

I looked down at the open notebook on my lap. A line of ink ran across the page, half-smudged where my hand had drifted in sleep.

Strength isn't the absence of fear. It's deciding to stay anyway.

I didn't remember writing it, but it sounded like something I needed to believe.

The air felt heavier this morning, the weight that only comes before change. The glow beneath my shirt pulsed once; faint, steady, blue again. Not the burning red of the Tower. Not the color of endings.

Change.

That was what Elias had said Death meant. Not destruction, but transformation. I wasn't sure which one I was closer to now.

I stood carefully, pulling the blanket over Serena's shoulders and wrapping it around her properly. She stirred, brow furrowing, but didn't wake. The sight made my chest ache; even in sleep, she looked like she was bracing for something.

Maybe she was. Perhaps we both were.

I crossed to the window and drew the curtain back just enough to let the dawn in. The first light spilled through, pale and cold, spilling through, catching on the frost. Outside, Havenbrook was still half-dreaming, no footsteps, no chapel bells yet, just the quiet exhale of winter.

I caught my reflection in the glass. For a moment, it was just me. Then, faintly, I saw the shimmer beneath my ribs: the shape of the card burning through like a heartbeat under ice.

Death, still there. Still mine.

But I wasn't afraid of it anymore. Not today.

Behind me, Serena shifted, mumbling something that sounded like my name. I turned, and for that moment, everything in me went still. The fear, the questions, the weight of what was coming, all of it quieted beneath the simple fact that she was here, and alive, and had chosen to stay.

I sat on the chair near the bed, my hand finding hers. Her fingers curled faintly around mine in her sleep.

"I don't know what's coming," I whispered. "But I'll face it. I swear it. For both of us."

The snow outside caught a little more light. The world began to wake; lamps dimming, the first bell ringing across the courtyard, distant but clear.

For the first time in a long while, it didn't sound like a warning.

Serena's grip tightened slightly, enough to pull me back from whatever thoughts started spiraling. I looked down at her and felt something small and steady settle in my chest.

Strength wasn't loud. It wasn't the kind of thing you shouted into the dark. It was this. Quiet. Chosen.

I brushed my thumb across her hand, and when the second bell rang, I whispered, barely more than breath—

"I'm still here."

The wind answered with a sigh against the window. The card in my chest pulsed once, slow and certain.

And for the first time since Elias died, I believed it.

Chapter 19: The Hermit

"Upright, the lantern burns… reversed, the lantern dies."

For a long time, I just watched Serena. The quiet between us felt sacred, unrepeatable.

Outside, snow kept falling. It wasn't heavy; more like ash drifting slowly through the morning light. The world felt muffled, distant, suspended. Somewhere below the dorm window, someone was shoveling paths through the courtyard, their scraping distant and rhythmically human.

I should've gotten up. I should've made coffee, checked the school messages, or pretended to start the day. But I didn't.

I just sat there, listening to the soft rise of her breath, the weight of her presence, and that strange, impossible peace.

I didn't think about cards, fate, or the shadow between worlds for once. I didn't think about Elias, the Tower, or the promise I had made.

I only thought: *If this is all I get, let it be enough.*

But peace never lasts long. Not for people like me.

It began with a dimming of the light. It was not a sudden eclipse; it was more like the world exhaling and forgetting to inhale again. The cold pressed closer. The air sharpened.

At first, I thought it was just another nightmare. Then I heard it: a voice like velvet cutting through glass.

"Still awake, little anchor?"

I froze.

The room wasn't dark exactly; it was colorless, drained of hue until everything was shadow and silver. The air felt like being underwater.

And there he was.

Nightmare stood at the foot of the bed, dressed like before. His hair shone like polished obsidian in the sun's gentle glow. He looked almost bored, the way only something ancient could look bored.

"Go away," I whispered.

"I could," he said mildly. "But I don't think you want that."

Serena stirred in her sleep, murmuring something, but didn't wake. The air around her shimmered faintly, as though she were sealed off from what was happening. Nightmare's gaze flicked toward her, then back to me.

"She dreams deeply," he said. "A rare gift. I envy her."

"Don't."

"Why not?" he asked. "Dreams are the only place where belief still dances without fear. The living world…it has grown so tired of pretending it understands itself."

I pushed myself upright, careful not to wake Serena. "You shouldn't be here."

He smiled faintly. "You said that the last time."

"And I meant it."

"Then consider this an uninvited courtesy call."

He stepped closer, hands clasped behind his back, posture refined. The shadows followed him like loyal dogs.

"You've been quiet lately," he said. "No questions. No fear."

"Guess I'm improving."

He studied me, eyes unreadable and gray as smoke. "Or surrendering."

I shook my head. "Living."

"Ah," he said softly. "That fragile word again."

He turned slightly, his attention wandering to the frost laced across the window. "Do you know why men build windows, Travis Calder?"

I frowned. "To see outside?"

"To convince themselves that the world beyond still exists," he said. "They cannot stand the idea of being alone in their walls."

"Then maybe that's why I keep mine open."

Nightmare smiled, thin and almost fond. "You are clever. Elias was right about that."

The name felt like a stone dropped into still water.

"Don't," I said.

"He would've wanted you to listen," Nightmare said. "He spent his last years trying to contain what you've become. You were his greatest success… and his greatest fear."

"He saved me."

"No," said Nightmare, voice velvet-soft but merciless. "He delayed you."

The glow beneath my chest flickered faintly, reacting to him. He watched it with a kind of reverence, then continued.

"You feel it, don't you? The tremor. The threads of the weave are loosening. You stand at the edge of unmaking, and yet you pretend at normalcy. Coffee. Class. Love." His eyes flicked toward Serena again. "You clutch at borrowed time."

"Because it's mine to clutch."

He tilted his head. "You still think you can keep it."

"I can live in it," I said.

"Until it falls apart."

"Then I'll build something new."

Nightmare's smile returned, patient and tired. "You speak like a godling who has not yet learned the cost of creation."

"I'm not a god," I said.

"No," he agreed. "You are worse. You are hope."

The word hit harder than I expected.

He took another step forward. The light bent around him, distorting slightly, like the air couldn't hold him properly. "The space between the weavings grows. Every disbelief widens it. Every act of rebellion against the pattern weakens it further. And still, you cling to this dream of living. Do you not see? You are part of the unraveling."

"Maybe the weave deserves to break," I said quietly.

Nightmare's eyes flashed with something like pride. "Now you begin to understand."

"I said maybe," I snapped.

He watched me for a long moment, expression unreadable. "You could join me," he said finally. "Stand at my side when the last belief falters. See what comes after. Truth unbound. Meaning unmade."

"I've seen what comes after," I said. "It looks a lot like loneliness."

Something passed across his face, the faintest flicker of memory. "Perhaps," he said. "But solitude is honest. Love is not."

I looked back at Serena, still asleep, her face turned toward the faint light of dawn. "You're wrong."

"Am I?" His voice lowered, almost gentle now. "What happens when the weave collapses? When belief dies? You'll watch her fade like smoke. You'll reach for her and find nothing. And I will still be here, waiting. I am patient, Travis Calder. Eternity has no rival in patience."

"Then wait," I said.

He paused, surprised again. I could feel it.

"You would rather burn in the delusion of warmth than embrace truth?"

"I'd rather love what's here than worship what's gone."

For the first time, Nightmare didn't reply right away. His gaze lingered on me; not cruel, not even superior. Just... curious. Like he was seeing something he didn't quite understand. Finally, he said, "You think your defiance makes you free."

"It makes me alive."

He looked at Serena again. "She will die."

"I know."

"And you will follow."

"I know."

He leaned closer, voice barely above a whisper. "And yet you smile."

"Because for once," I said, "it doesn't matter what the cards say."

Silence fell between us, the kind that isn't empty, but full.

Then Nightmare straightened his posture, gloved hands folding neatly again. "You remind me of him," he said softly.

"Elias?"

"No. The first one who defied the weave." His expression darkened. "He called himself human, too."

I swallowed. "What happened to him?"

Nightmare smiled faintly. "He learned that faith and doubt are the same thread, twisted backward. You will, too."

He stepped back, and the air began to distort. His outline flickered, edges bleeding into shadow. Before he vanished, his voice brushed against my mind, smooth and cold:

"When the silence comes, little anchor, remember that you could have been eternal."

The shadows folded inward. The light returned.

The room felt too quiet. The world is too small. I sat there for a long while, staring at the space where he had been, until my pulse stopped echoing in my ears.

Serena stirred. Her eyes opened, sleepy, soft. "You okay?" she murmured.

I nodded slowly. "Yeah," I said. "Just thinking."

She smiled faintly, still half-asleep, and turned over. Within seconds, her breathing evened out again. I sat there until the first real sunlight broke through the window. The card in my chest glowed faintly, not red or blue, but shining. I understood what it meant for the first time in a long time. Not death. Not return. Just living in the brief and fragile middle of it all.

And for now, that was enough

Chapter 20: Temperance

"Upright, harmony restored... reversed, harmony broken."

The chapel bells rang early that morning; soft, unhurried, as if even sound had learned to retake its time.

Serena and I walked together through the frost-lined courtyard, our breath visible in the thin morning light. The air had that crisp, clean stillness that only happens after the first thaw: everything damp and bright, as though the world had been washed overnight.

She wore my scarf again, wrapped three times around her neck. "You realize," she said, "this is basically an admission that I look better in your clothes than you do."

"Conceded," I said as I interlocked her fingers with mine.

We cut across the courtyard where the last snow clung stubbornly to the hedges. Students trickled toward the chapel doors, their chatter low and drowsy; the stained glass caught the morning sun, scattering fragments of color across the cobblestone.

That was when I saw three figures standing near the steps, mid-conversation.

Grant, still getting used to the freedom from the sling, gestured as he spoke. Lena was beside him, her coat buttoned to the chin and her hands tucked into her pockets. And Chloe, always composed and sharp, though there was a softness to her now that hadn't been there before.

Grant saw us first and waved, an easy, genuine motion that caught me off guard.

"Travis!" he called. "Hey."

"Hey, yourself," I said as we reached them. The air between us didn't feel strained anymore, just careful. "You look better."

"Feels better," he said, rolling his shoulder. "Guess time does fix some things."

Lena smiled faintly. "And other things just learn to coexist."

"Profound as always," Serena said with a grin.

"Law student," Lena said. "It's a coping mechanism."

Chloe regarded me with her usual tremendous curiosity. "Haven't seen you much this semester."

"Been… recalibrating," I said.

Her lips quirked. "Good word for it."

Grant nodded toward the chapel. "You going in?"

"Wouldn't miss it," Serena said. "Nate's leading, right?"

"Yeah," Lena said. "He's gotten good at it. Even learned to keep it under thirty minutes."

"That's a miracle," Chloe murmured.

We laughed, and the tension, whatever was left, cracked and dissolved. The six of us stood there for a moment, awkwardly but sincerely together, like people who had all survived different storms and finally found themselves under the same patch of calm sky.

"Listen," I said, glancing between them. "I wanted to say, thank you. For being patient with me. I know I didn't make that easy."

Grant shrugged. "You owned it. That's more than most."

Lena nodded. "The rest of us aren't exactly saints."

Chloe smiled, just slightly. "Some of us more than others."

Serena nudged me. "See? Harmony. You should write this down. It won't last forever."

"Realist," I said.

"Artist," she corrected.

The chapel doors opened behind us, and the soft hum of the organ began. Light filtered through the stained glass in fractured golds and blues. Grant gestured toward the entrance. "Shall we?"

We filed in together, slipping into pews halfway down the aisle. The smell of wax and pine polish filled the air, grounding, familiar. The light from the windows painted shifting shapes across the stone floor, saints and stars, patience and promise.

Nate stood at the pulpit, posture easy but assured. He looked like someone who'd found his rhythm: confident, humble, genuinely present. When he saw Serena and me, he smiled briefly and then began.

"Today's reading," he said, "isn't about answers. It's about balance."

The word struck me immediately: balance. Temperance.

He spoke simply, but there was weight to his voice: about holding contradictions, faith, and doubt as necessary halves of understanding, about living with the tension instead of trying to erase it.

As he talked, my gaze wandered to Serena just across the aisle from me, head slightly bowed; to Grant, hands folded neatly in his lap, to Lena and Chloe whispering about something that made them both smile. For the first time, the chapel didn't feel like a place of questions. It felt like a place of breathing.

When the final hymn faded, Nate stepped down, shaking hands as people filed past him. The crowd spilled out into the sunlight, the air full of low chatter and the clink of coffee cups from the tables outside.

Serena and I lingered a little, talking with Maya and David near the back pews. Maya had somehow smuggled in a muffin and was eating it unapologetically.

"I maintain," she said between bites, "that sermons hit harder with carbs."

David rolled his eyes. "You're why they post 'no food or drink' signs."

"I'm a martyr for flavor," Maya said solemnly.

Serena laughed. "And caffeine."

"Obviously."

Maya leaned back against the pew, grinning. "So. Word around campus says you two are official as well."

Serena raised an eyebrow. "Word around campus has a fast mouth."

David smirked. "Translation: Maya spread the news fast."

I tried not to smile. Failed. "Yeah," I said quietly. "We figured."

Maya whooped loud enough to startle an old woman near the aisle. "Finally!"

Serena hid her blush behind a mock glare. "You are insufferable."

"Professionally," Maya said.

I laughed, and it didn't feel like I was trying to sound okay. I just was.

We stayed there a while, just talking, catching up, letting the morning stretch lazily into the afternoon. Maya told us about her latest article draft ("A Theological Critique of Cafeteria Coffee"); David countered with a story about accidentally locking himself in the theology archives for two hours.

By the time we stepped outside, the sun had begun its descent, warming the stone steps. Students crossed the courtyard in clusters, laughter bouncing off the chapel walls. The air smelled faintly of thaw and promise.

That was when I saw him.

Victor stood near the fountain, coat buttoned to the throat, hair caught by the wind. He looked almost the same, calm, unreadable, but something gentler in how his shoulders held themselves.

He noticed me, then Serena. His eyes lingered on her for a moment before settling on me again.

“Travis,” he said.

“Victor.”

“Can we talk?”

I looked at Serena. She nodded once. “I’ll wait by the café,” she said softly, and slipped away.

Victor and I walked in silence across the courtyard. The path to the philosophy hall was familiar now, the stones uneven but steady. We climbed to the roof again, our unlikely meeting place, and stood at the edge, where the world seemed to open.

The wind carried the last notes of a distant bell.

“You look different,” he said.

“I feel different.”

“I can tell.” He glanced toward the horizon. “You saw him again, didn’t you?”

“Just this morning.”

He nodded slowly. “Nightmare.”

"Yes."

"And?"

I exhaled. "He offered again. To join him. To help unmake the weave. To see the truth."

"And you said?"

I smiled faintly. "No."

Victor's expression didn't change immediately. Then, slowly, something like confusion touched it.

"He didn't take that well, I imagine."

"No," I said. "But he understood. Or at least pretended to."

Victor chuckled softly. "You always manage to disarm even the cosmic horrors."

"I told him I chose to live," I said simply. "To love. To stay here until the world ends, if it must."

He studied me for a long moment. "That's braver than it sounds."

"I don't know about brave. Maybe just tired of running."

"Same thing sometimes."

The wind tugged at his coat. Below us, the campus gleamed in the moon's early light, familiar, fragile, alive. The last of the snow melted into thin silver lines down the roof.

"He said the world will fall," I said. "That disbelief will swallow belief. That silence comes for everything."

Victor nodded. "Maybe it will. But you'll still have lived in it. That's more than most people manage."

"I used to think I needed to find meaning," I said. "Now I just want to keep it company."

"That," Victor said quietly, "is meaning."

We stood there in silence. The clouds shifted. I could feel the warmth of sunlight breaking through, faint but real.

Down below, Serena crossed the courtyard, her scarf bright against the pale ground. Victor followed my gaze. His mouth softened into a small smile.

"She suits you," he said.

"She saves me," I replied.

He nodded. "Then maybe she's your card after all."

I looked at him. "You don't believe in the cards."

"I don't," he said. "But belief's never been the point, has it?"

"No," I said, smiling. "I guess not."

He reached into his pocket and pulled something small and silver: a coin, worn smooth on one side. "Keep this," he said, pressing it into my palm. "For luck. Or disbelief. Whichever works."

I looked down at it, then back up, but he was already walking toward the stairs.

"Victor," I called.

He turned.

"Thank you," I said.

He nodded once, hands in his pockets, and disappeared down the stairwell.

I stayed there a while, watching the sky, the students, the slow rhythm of a world still turning.

When I finally returned, Serena was waiting at the base of the steps, two coffees in hand. She handed me one.

"How'd it go?" she asked.

"He understood," I said. "More than I thought he would."

She smiled, the kind that warmed from the inside out. "Then maybe that's what balance looks like."

"Maybe," I said.

We walked together through the courtyard, and the snow finally melted into the soil. The air was soft and new. The chapel bell rang again behind us; slow, steady, patient.

The world didn't feel fixed. But it felt whole.

And for once, that was enough.

Chapter 21: The World

"When upright, The World means completion, unity, and fulfillment... yet, reversed, it warns of delays, emptiness, and unfinished journeys."

The house stood on the lake's edge, quiet, small, and patient.

It was once a summer cabin, built from weathered pine and glass. Over the years, Serena painted the walls in the color of soft smoke and filled the rooms with sketches, books, and old photographs. The deck looked out over the still water, where the light curved in gentle ripples.

It was late summer, the air cool enough to bite at dusk, and the crickets had begun their slow symphony outside the open windows.

Serena sat by the window with a cup of tea, wrapped in an old sweater that hung loose around her shoulders. Her hair had gone silver, streaked rather than faded, and her eyes still carried the same warmth that once made even the darkest nights bearable.

"You're staring," she said, not looking up.

"I'm memorizing," I replied.

She smiled. "I've told you before: memory never listens to requests."

"True," I said, settling into the armchair opposite her. "But I can try."

The lamp between us glowed softly, and a slight halo of gold was around our quiet.

Outside, the lake mirrored the fading sky, pale blue gave way to lavender, and deep indigo.

We had been retired for a decade now. Havenbrook was far behind us, though sometimes I still dreamed of its courtyards, the chapel's bell, the taste of burnt coffee from Crown Café.

Serena still painted, though less often. I still taught, now and then, when the local college begged me to cover a guest lecture on mythic symbology or "nonlinear theology." I always refused to call it mysticism. She always laughed when I did.

"Do you ever think," she said, "about what it would've been like if Elias hadn't found you?"

"All the time," I said.

"And?"

"I'd probably still be asking the same questions. Just louder."

She chuckled, shaking her head. “You never did learn how to rest.”

“I’m resting now.”

“Are you?”

I looked out toward the lake. The surface caught the first shimmer of starlight. “I think so. The questions don’t burn anymore. They hum. Like background music.”

“That’s progress,” she said, sipping her tea.

We sat in silence, belonging to people who have shared too much life and need words.

After a while, she said, “Do you ever miss it? The cards?”

I hesitated. “Sometimes. Not what they did, but what they represented. They gave everything shape. Meaning.”

“And now?”

“Now I think meaning doesn’t need a shape,” I said. “It just needs a heartbeat.”

She smiled faintly. “That sounds like something Elias would’ve said.”

“Maybe. But Elias would’ve charged tuition for it.”

That earned me a laugh, the kind that still softened the world's edges. The clock ticked gently in the corner. Outside, the wind shifted through the trees, carrying the faint scent of rain.

"I've been thinking," she said.

"That's dangerous."

"Very," she agreed. "But hear me out. We always talked about fate, about whether it binds or frees. About how belief and disbelief shape everything." She set her cup down. "What if both were wrong? What if it's neither binding nor freeing? What if it just is?"

I leaned back, considering. "Existence as an act of balance."

"Temperance," she said.

"Full circle."

She smiled. "Exactly."

Her gaze drifted toward the old bookshelf, where our physical cards still sat in their worn leather box. We hadn't touched them in years. They were relics now, not tools.

"Do you think," she asked softly, "that G-d minds we stopped using them?"

"No," I said. "I think He prefers we learn to walk without the railings."

She nodded slowly. "Freedom, then."

"Freedom," I echoed.

The room is filled with sacred quiet, not because of prayer, but because of presence.

After a while, she said, "Travis?"

"Hmm?"

"Read me."

I blinked. "What?"

She pointed to her chest. "Just once more. For fun."

"Serena..."

"Please," she said, voice gentle but insistent. "It's been years."

"I don't think—"

"Don't think," she said, smiling. "Just look."

I sighed, shaking my head. "You've always known how to make an argument sound holy."

"It's one of my gifts," she said.

So I looked.

Old habit stirred like a half-remembered song. The world softened at the edges. The air took on that faint shimmer I used to see when the veil thinned.

And there it was.

The faint, steady glow at the center of her chest was soft blue, calm, and complete.

But it wasn't a card I recognized at first. The lines had shifted, curved, intertwined. Then they settled, forming the image clear as water:

The World.

The final arcana. Completion. Wholeness. The dance that binds beginning to ending, and ending to starting again.

She watched me quietly. "What do you see?"

"The end," I said softly. "And everything that came before it."

Her eyes shone in the lamplight. "Good."

I took her hand, tracing the lines of her palm, as I used to when we were students, nervous, uncertain, on the cusp of everything.

"You know," she said after a while, "we were so afraid of destiny back then. So desperate to defy it."

"And we did," I said.

"Did we?"

"We lived," I said. "That's all defiance ever was."

Her thumb brushed over my knuckles. "I'm glad we never had children."

I looked up, surprised.

She smiled faintly. "I mean it. We would've loved them, of course. But this… this quiet… It's ours. It's enough."

I nodded. "It is."

Outside, the first stars shimmered, reflected perfectly in the lake, two worlds, above and below, mirroring one another.

Serena leaned back in her chair, closing her eyes. "Do you think we'll ever see them again?"

"The cards?"

She smiled. "Elias. The others. Victor."

I thought about that for a long moment. "If there's a weave still left, then maybe. If not…"

"If not?"

"Then maybe they're already here," I said. "In what we built. In the quiet."

She opened her eyes again and looked at me. "That's a nice thought."

"It's yours," I said. "You gave it to me years ago."

We sat there until the lamp burned low, the world dimming into the hush of late night.

Before we turned in, I glanced again at her, the faint blue glow still pulsing beneath her skin.

The World.

And for the first time, I realized it wasn't prophecy. It was gratitude.

We went to bed hand in hand. I didn't wonder what the cards might say next. I didn't care.

The wind shifted sometime after midnight.

I woke to a low, humming whisper against the windowpanes; soft enough not to wake Serena, but steady enough to call me from sleep.

The room was awash in silver. The moonlight pooled across the floorboards, tracing the outlines of the old desk, the shelves, the familiar coat draped over the chair. The air was still before dawn, when even time seemed to hold its breath.

Serena slept soundly beside me, one arm curled beneath her cheek. The glow beneath her skin, The World, pulsed faintly as it began to fade.

I sat up, careful not to wake her. My reflection in the window was faint, blurred by moonlight, but there was still the old shimmer beneath my ribs: softer now, not the searing red it once was, but something muted, gentle, like embers that had learned patience.

I just watched the lake outside for a while; flat, silver, endless.

And then the light in the corner of the room began to change.

It didn't brighten or flicker; it deepened like the shadows were folding inward, rearranging themselves into something almost human.

When the shape took form, I thought I recognized him immediately when the shape took form, but it was not Nightmare.

The figure stood tall, his outline softened by the moonlight, his posture easy, unthreatening. He wore a white shirt, the sleeves rolled to his forearms, and simple trousers. His hair was dark but streaked with gray, and his face was calm; not empty, but profoundly still, like a man who'd been walking a long time and finally found a place to rest.

"Good evening, Travis," he said, his voice carrying the weight of both silence and memory.

I didn't move. "Nightmare?"

He smiled, faintly. "Not quite. My name is William."

I blinked. "You look... human."

"Disappointing, isn't it?" he said, almost amused. "After all the smoke and terror. I suppose I could dress the part, but I find honesty easier in this shape."

I swung my legs over the edge of the bed, bare feet on the wooden floor. "You're real, then."

"As real as you," he said. "Perhaps more so, in certain lights."

Serena stirred slightly beside me. He looked toward her and smiled, not how a predator studies prey, but how a teacher might look upon a well-written poem. "She dreams of color," he said softly. "Always has."

I swallowed. "You said your name is William."

He nodded. "That's what I was called before the spaces began. Before belief fractured and made room for creatures like your friend Nightmare."

"So you knew him."

"I knew him very well," William repeated, amused. "We were partnered together after my mother passed. He is the echo of disbelief; I am now the residue of faith. We are the twins of choice, the two halves that hold the weave apart."

I frowned. "Then why come to me?"

"Because you've walked between us," he said simply. "Because you learned to hold both without breaking."

"I didn't learn," I said quietly. "I survived."

"That's learning," he said. "It's just the unfortunately hard kind."

The wind outside picked up, threading through the trees. The air shimmered faintly, not with heat, but with a kind of gentle luminescence, like starlight bent into the shape of memory.

William walked closer to the window, his bare feet making no sound. He looked out over the lake. "You've done well, you know. You've lived."

"I tried," I said.

"No," he said softly. "You chose. That's rarer."

He turned toward me, hands in his pockets. "Do you remember what Nightmare told you? About disbelief making the gaps?"

"Yes."

"He was right, in his way," William said. "But he misunderstood what fills those gaps. It isn't void. It's mercy."

I blinked. "Mercy?"

He smiled. "Every place where belief falters, kindness slips in. Doubt doesn't destroy faith; it humbles it. That's what holds the world together, Travis. Not the cards. Not the weave. Mercy."

The word settled into me like a heartbeat finding its rhythm again.

I looked down at the faint light still glowing beneath my ribs. "Why are you here, then? To give me more answers?"

"No," he said. "To tell you it's enough."

Its simplicity hit harder than any revelation could.

He stepped closer, close enough that I could see the faint lines at the corners of his eyes; not wrinkles, but marks of time. "I am the other one Nightmare spoke of," he said quietly. "The other side of the same truth. Where he offers collapse, I offer return."

"Return to what?"

"To peace," he said. "When you and Serena are ready."

My throat tightened. "You mean—"

He shook his head. "Not yet. You still have days left, laughter, and all the quiet mornings that make meaning out of breath. But when the hour comes, you'll see me again. I will be waiting, with open arms."

The words should have scared me. They didn't. Something about his tone, gentle, patient, made me believe him. He moved toward the door, his shape beginning to fade, dissolving into the same silver light that had formed him.

"William," I said.

He paused.

"Was Elias right?"

He smiled faintly. "About what?"

"About death not being an ending."

William turned slightly, the faintest glint of moonlight catching his profile. "He was close," he said. "It's not an ending. It's a beginning."

He began to fade again, the edges of him thinning like mist. "Rest, Travis. You've carried the world long enough."

"Will we see you soon?" I asked.

"When you're ready," he said. "You'll know the way."

And then he was gone.

The room was still again. The moonlight returned to being just moonlight. I looked at Serena; her breath was even, her expression soft, and she was asleep.

I lay beside her, tracing the edge of her hand with mine until our fingers intertwined. The faint blue glow had already disappeared, as did mine. Outside, the lake caught the first reflection of dawn. The two worlds, water and sky, blurred until they were indistinguishable. For a long while, I simply breathed. When I finally closed my eyes, the silence wasn't empty. It was whole.

1

www.ingramcontent.com/pod-product-compliance
Lightning Source LLC
La Vergne TN
LVHW010657110826
845149LV00014B/3125

* 9 7 8 1 9 7 1 2 7 3 0 0 6 *